This book is dedicated to rising taxes, broken promises, forgotten children, crime, starvation, war, death, and despair.

Thanks for the inspiration, guys. Couldn't have done it without you.

AVARITIA

A FABLE

M.D. WESTBROOK

M.W. Publishers

In a house lived a mother, a father, and two brothers.

The younger brother owned three rats.

Across the hallway, the older brother kept multiple families of mice in a glass tank on a bookshelf.

The rats were pets.

The mice, unfortunately, were not . . .

Chapter 1

A Life Hard to Stomach

"**N**ot me! Not me! Please! Cookie, help!" Radish squeaked as her frail body was lifted into the air, out of the glass tank.

A mouse with tan fur, dotted with chocolate-chip-like spots, leapt up and clung to Radish, trying to pull her free from the iron grip of Older Brother Human.

"Hold on, Radish! Hold on! It will be okay!" Cookie squeaked, dangling from his mate.

"Get off her, you," Older Brother Human chuckled, shaking Cookie loose.

The wood shavings cushioned his fall, and in a flash Cookie was back on his feet. The chocolate-chip spotted mouse ran forward and pounded on the glass wall, clumps of Radish's fur stuck between his claws. "Take me! Take me and leave her!"

Older Brother Human lifted Radish over a separate container where a large monster, longer than forty mice, flicked its black tongue.

The snake had caught Radish's scent.

"No! No! No!" Cookie tried climbing out of the prison to rescue his mate, but his claws only clicked rapidly against the glass. Other mice rushed forward and pulled Cookie back before he hurt himself.

Older Brother Human dropped Radish into the snake's container, and a hush came over the mice as they watched the horrifying scene unfold.

Radish caught sight of the snake coiled around a broken branch, and scurried to the opposite corner of the tank. Like Cookie, she clawed against the glass, desperate to escape, but no grip could be found. Radish's pleas for help were muffled.

Cookie cried uncontrollably, watching as the snake slithered behind his mate.

In a blink, the snake struck. Radish released a final squeak as the constrictor wrapped around her lower abdomen.

"Noooo!" Cookie wailed.

Radish opened her mouth, gasping, and beat her tiny paws against the orange and yellow scales, but to no avail. Radish's once soft pink eyes bulged, now a darker hue of red.

Older Brother Human laughed out loud. "Good boy, Petey. Eat 'er up."

As the snake's grip grew tighter, Radish's voracious scratching had slowed to a sporadic twitch in her right paw. Her mouth gaped open. She stared into nothingness.

A few seconds later, even the twitching had ceased.

She was dead.

The snake loosened its hold, and Radish's corpse dropped into the wood shavings. Starting from the head, the snake slowly gulped down her body until Radish's tail hung from its mouth like a long, pink tongue.

The human became bored and left the room, leaving his door open.

Cookie collapsed into the wood flakes, muttering, "Not Radish. Not Radish. Not Radish . . ."

The other mice gathered around Cookie and gave squeaks of comfort.

"Don't worry, Cookie. Her pain is over."

"She lasted longer than most, Cookie."

"At least she went knowing you loved her."

York, an elderly mouse with white and black peppered fur, made his way closest to Cookie.

"I know what it's like, Cookie. With time, it will pass," York muttered as he put a paw on the widower's shoulder. "It will pass."

The words he spoke were true, and indeed, if anyone was well acquainted with death, it was York. York's own mate had been gobbled up a month ago, only a few weeks after the birth of their second litter of pups. Naturally, York loved all fifteen of his babes, but there was little he could do to protect them from the human's grasping hand during Feeding Time. One by one, he had watched his darling sons and daughters have the life squeezed from their bodies. Out of the fifteen babes, only nine remained.

York turned to the crowd of mouse families. "We honor those who make the sacrifice. Another day to eat. Another day to sleep. What a glory to give your all for fellow mice."

Before York had finished, every mouse had joined in, for they also knew the saying by heart. Even Cookie sputtered the last sentence in mournful sobs.

As the mice bowed their heads for a moment of silence, York felt a tug on his fur. He looked down at Hazel, his youngest, snuggled against his side.

"What?" he whispered.

Hazel pointed to a mouse unnoticed by the rest, sitting off in a corner of the tank, not participating. He had black fur, black eyes, and even a tinted black tail.

York gritted his fangs in anger. "Not again, Benny."

"Why do you do this, Benny? Do you want the attention? Is that it? Don't you realize what the others are starting to think of you? What they are starting to think of me?"

The black mouse babe did not respond and only continued to gaze through the glass and across the hallway.

York sighed. "You have to stop this obsession, Benny. You have to forget your mother's stories of The Wild. It's been weeks. She's . . . she's gone now."

Again, Benny did not respond.

"Please, Benny, for once will you listen to me?"

Benny turned and looked up into his father's eyes.

The action caught York by surprise, but he straightened his back and stroked his whiskers. "It's time you accept reality, Benny." He pointed to the wood-flake bedding with a claw. "*This* is our world. Not out there. One day, the human will feed you to the snake. It could be today; it could be tomorrow, so you might as well enjoy the time you have left. Because after that, there's nothing. Go eat, run in the wheel, play a game of chase . . . anything! Just stop," he waved his paws at Benny, "*this*."

"But they could help us," Benny squeaked softly.

"Help us? Who? The rats? Why would they ever want to help us?"

"I saw one, yesterday, when Mother Human went into Younger Brother Human's room."

"You saw one? A rat?" York crossed his paws. "All the way across the hall in the other room?"

"Yes."

"Did they see you?"

"I think so. She had—"

"She?"

"Yes, I'm sure it was a she, and I . . . I waved to her."

"And did she wave back?"

"No."

"So she didn't see you."

"No. She saw me," said Benny. "I know she did."

"Let me get this straight: you think the rats, who are given food, shelter, and are *not* fed to a snake, are going to miraculously escape

4

their own cage, risk their lives, and come over here and save us. All because you waved at them?"

Instead of answering, Benny turned and went back to staring through the glass.

"Benny?"

Benny did not answer.

"Fine. Be like that." York began to stomp away, but turned and shouted, "It's time you wake up to reality, Benny!"

Chapter 2

Routine

The next day, the mice did the usual. They ate. They pooped. They ran in their wheel. They slept.

Benny pondered his father's words and soon gave up trying to see the rats. His father was right. He was going to die here.

Benny cried himself to sleep.

Chapter 3

Moving Socks

"**G**et up."

Benny moaned and snuggled down deeper into the wood shavings.

A large bolt of lightning shot up his tail, but before Benny could squeak in pain, a leatherly tail slapped against his mouth.

Benny found himself staring into the black piercing eyes of a rat. The creature was at least three times Benny's size with sleek, black fur, its snout long and pointy.

"Hush, Mouse. Not a peep. Just do what you're told like the rest." The creature's voice sounded like two grinding stones.

Glancing over the rat's shoulder, Benny realized the glass tank was alive with movement in the dark. Shadowy figures of mice huddled in a corner of the tank. In this corner stood another large rat, a female with white fur and gray spots. She stood on her hind legs, placing her forepaws against the glass wall. Mice were climbing up the rat's back like a ladder towards an opening where the plastic lid had been shifted.

"We are leaving. Now," the black rat growled. He removed his tail from Benny's mouth and joined the white rat in helping mice over the tank's edge.

The group of mice waiting to climb the "rat ladder" to freedom were whispering excitedly as they waited their turn, but a harsh glare from the black rat quickly hushed them. After a few more nervous minutes, it was Benny's turn.

"Last one," the black male rat muttered to the white rat acting as the ladder.

"You sure they are worth it?" she whispered back.

"The Old Code, Dolley." This statement seemed to satisfy her, for no more was said between the two.

The black rat shoved him forward. "Your turn."

Benny began climbing up Dolley's back. Her white fur was slick and thin. As Benny stood on the rat's shoulders, reaching for the edge of the tank, his foot-paw slipped and grazed against the left side of her face.

"Sorry," Benny whispered. Looking down, he was afraid he had poked Dolley in the eye with his paw. However, she had no eye to poke. It was an empty socket, bridging a scar that ran across her brow and cheek, evidence of a past wound.

The right eye, however, worked just fine and glared up at Benny. "Move it, now!" she hissed.

Benny pulled himself up and shifted his weight forward. He landed on his back, and the wind was knocked from him.

Benny felt a paw help him up. It belonged to a third rat. She was the youngest of the three and not much larger than Benny. She had white fur, complete with a large black spot encircling her left eye.

Benny recognized her. She was the rat he had waved at two days ago. "Um. Hi."

Before she could respond, the rat whirled around. "Watch out!"

Humphrey's son, Crumb, had wondered off and was tottering dangerously close to the bookshelf's edge, but his father had not noticed, too busy whispering with the others in excitement.

"Oh, for the Ancients' sake—"The rat lunged forward and grabbed Crumb by the tail just as the babe began to lose his balance and totter off the side.

She dragged Crumb next to Humphrey and hissed, "Will you keep control of your babe!"The rat turned her attention back to Benny and pointed a claw to the group of mice. "Stop gawking and get over here."

Benny did.

"I swear, it's like trying to herd cockroaches," she mumbled.

Dolley climbed out of the cage and approached the younger rat. "Moon, your father says for us to go on. He will catch up."

The young rat, Moon, gave a nod, and her authoritative voice changed to that of respect. "Yes, Mother."

Dolley turned to the group of mice and whispered, "Now listen up. You're going to follow my daughter single file towards the exit near the electric socket. There, Rose will be waiting for you."

Humphrey's eyes lit up. "Rose? My mate, Rose? She's helping you?"

Rose was an amber furred mouse who had broken into tears one night after fighting with Humphrey. Her squeaks of sorrow woke Older Brother Human.

"That's it. You're snake food," the human had muttered, lifting her out of the tank.

However, too lazy to turn on his lights, the human tripped over a pile of clothes and lost his hold on Rose. Humphrey's mate was able to escape through the same hole near the electric outlet the rat had just mentioned. Since then, Rose had not been seen or heard of.

"Yes, and if you want to be reunited, do as you're told." Dolley turned to her daughter. "Lead them, Moon."

Moon gave another nod. "Yes, Mother." And, as quick as a flash, she was off. The young rat leapt off the bookshelf and onto the computer desk. Then, she leapt again onto the armrest of the swivel chair. From there, she scurried down the chair to the carpeted floor.

The mice were only used to the wood-flake bedding beneath their paws, and seeing the dangerous path, hesitated to follow.

Benny took a few steps back, ran forward and leapt off the shelf. His natural reflexes kicked in, and he easily landed on the desk. Seeing the young mouse effortlessly perform the feat sparked confidence in the other mice. One by one, they jumped off the shelf and onto the desk, following Benny.

When Benny reached the carpet, Moon was already halfway across the bedroom floor.

For Benny, running so far and so fast unrestricted felt exhilarating. Any moment, he felt as if he would bump his snout into a glass wall.

Suddenly, there was a loud squeak, and all froze. One of the mice had slipped off the swivel chair and fallen several feet to the floor.

Older Brother Human snored on.

The fallen mouse rolled over, brushed his whiskers, and joined the line, limping.

Benny saw Moon roll her eyes at the clumsiness before continuing on. They reached the hole in the wall and Benny crawled through first, fighting the urge to sneeze from the drywall dust.

"Benny, is that you?"

"Rose?"

"Did Crumb make it?"

"I . . . I think so."

"Oh, thank goodness. And Humphrey?"

Benny nodded.

"Oh . . ." Her whiskers drooped.

Benny wanted to ask Rose what was wrong, but unfortunately, the two could not continue the conversation, for more mice began to enter through the hole and crowd inside the wall.

Half the mice had made it through when the ground began to shake.

Footsteps.

The door swung open and an explosion of light flooded in from the hallway.

"Hey, Trenton, you have to get up for basketball. And what did I tell you about leaving your socks on the—"

But then again, socks didn't move on their own.

Mother Human screamed, and the room broke out into chaos.

The single line of mice disintegrated as they charged towards the hole, clawing at the drywall, squeezing in two to three at a time.

Panicking, Rose did not wait for the rest of the mice. She turned and ran down the narrow pathway, squeaking loudly, "Follow me!"

Benny heard Older Brother Human's voice. "What, Mom? What is it—oh, crap!" A pair of feet came stomping down near the bed, almost crushing poor Humphrey.

Seeing the hole clogged with mice, Dolley squeaked, "One at a time! One at a time, you stupid creatures!"

Dolley gave the mice a large shove, and they tumbled through the hole, leaving just her and her mate in the open with the humans. Dolley turned, searching for the black rat, only to discover the outstretched hand of Older Brother Human reaching towards her.

"Got yo—*aaah!*"

Older Brother Human flipped onto his back, grasping his ankle. The large black rat clung to the boy's flesh with his fangs. The boy swatted the rat with the back of his hand, sending the creature flying against the swivel chair. The rat shook his head, and in a black blur, made his way around the boy and into the hole where Dolley and his daughter waited.

Benny had watched the whole spectacle in awe.

"What are you waiting for," the black rat growled, licking the blood from his broken snout. "Get going. Follow Rose or we'll be lost in here."

They did, through cracks and corners, over dust, and rusted nails, with the humans' shouts muffled on the other side of the drywall.

"My rats are gone, too!" cried Younger Brother Human.

"They must be in the walls."

"I knew this was gonna happen when I bought you kids those stupid rodents," shouted Father Human. "I knew this was gonna happen!

Rachel, go get the number for pest control!"

"Will he kill my rats? Don't let him kill my rats!"

Rose led the rats and the cage-mice into the crawl space under the house. From there, they scuttled along the top of a copper water pipe, which led to the garden faucet. Like the electric socket, there was a gap between the copper pipe and the wood siding of the house, just wide enough for a mouse and rat to slip through.

Benny tumbled into the fresh morning air and onto the dew-slick grass.

"Oh, there's one. Hurry, help him up."

Multiple paws lifted Benny off the ground, and he found himself face-to-face with mice he had never met.

Out of the group of strangers, the oldest mouse Benny had ever seen hobbled up to him, using a small, broken twig as a cane. His fur was dark gray. One of his eyes was covered with a thick cataract. Both of his front incisor teeth were missing, causing his occasional squeak to whistle. "You! Youngster! Are you Benny?"

Benny nodded.

"Follow me. Your father is looking for you."

The old mouse led Benny to a nearby rosebush where his newly freed friends and family were intermingled with more of these new strangers. The strangers shook the paws of the cage-mice, congratulating them on their escape. Benny's father and siblings were near the base of the rosebush. His brothers and sisters were already squealing with delight as they climbed the lower branches of the bush, playing a game of chase with their newfound friends.

York gave his son a strong hug. "I was worried about you. Can you believe it? We're free. We're free! I knew this day would come!"

Benny decided to ignore his father's last statement, and instead, asked: "Who are these mice?"

The elderly mouse who had led Benny to his father raised a bushy eyebrow. "I'm surprised Rose never mentioned us. We are wall-mice. You may address me as 'Lint'."

"Lint? That's a strange name, even for a mouse," said York.

The old mouse chuckled. "Got that name 'cause of the color of my fur. When I was a babe, Mother Human caught me behind the washing machine. Right there, that would have been the end of my short life, but she thought I was just a ball of lint and left me be."

"So, Rose has been living with you?"

Lint gave a nod. "Since the first night of her escape. See that fellow over there?" Lint pointed with his stick-cane to a dark brown mouse watching Rose hug Humphrey. "That's Pine. He showed Rose how to scrounge. If it weren't for Pine, she would have been a goner. Yep, if we wall-mice listen to anyone, it's Pine."

Benny noticed the large male rat drop from the hole. His mate and daughter guided him to a pair of tulips, away from the mice. Moon tore a leaf from a tulip and gave it to her father, who held it up against his bleeding snout.

Lint took notice of the rats as well. "Rats? Rats! Rose never mentioned rats! Pine, come here."

The leader of the wall-mice walked over, and Lint pointed in the direction of the tulips. "Did you know about this?"

"I think Rose mentioned it to me, yes," said the brown mouse calmly.

"And you didn't tell the rest of the clan?" growled Lint.

Pine scratched an ear and shrugged. "Just passed my mind, I guess. I don't see them hurting anyone."

Lint smacked his gums and jabbed his cane into the dirt repeatedly, too furious for words.

York nodded. "I agree. What does it matter? We're free!"

"Yes," shouted Cookie, wrapping his paws around his own babes. And for the first time since his mate's death, Cookie smiled. "We're free!"

Soon, the word *freedom* was on every mouse's lips, and they shouted it again and again, "Freedom! Freedom! Freedom!" Even quiet Benny began to take up the chant.

The family of rats did not join in.

The cheering turned to singing (though it sounded more like a chaos of squeaks), which York led in his deep bass voice:

No more snake and no more cage.
Left the humans in a rage.
We gained new lives with our wit,
and under blue skies we now sit
In freedom! In freedom!

Let it be so all can hear,
we will live together without fear.
Let weak and old live long days,
by charity and kind ways.
For freedom! For freedom!

As they repeated the verses again and again, babes began to skip and hop to the tune. The dancing, singing, and laughing could have gone on for hours . . . but the male rat made his way into the center, still holding the tulip leaf against his snout, a scowl on his face. The singing ceased, and a clearing opened up in the center as mice backed away, intimidated by the rat's size and serious demeanor.

The rat removed the leaf from his snout, gave his whiskers a twitch, and spoke: "I don't care what you do. But we follow The Old Code, and we escaped the humans so we could, in peace, teach our babes its ways."

"What happens if we don't believe in your Old Code?" asked Cookie.

The black rat merely shrugged. "It doesn't bother me one bit."

The rat exited the crowd, rejoined his family, and the three left the cover of the tulips and began crossing the lawn.

"What do you think, Pine?" York asked, watching the rats. "Should we follow them?"

"Uh, well . . ." Pine didn't seem to know the answer himself. "They do seem like they know where they're going."

"Maybe if we just followed them for a little bit," suggested York. "The cage-mice will follow my lead. Do you wall-mice agree?"

"Rats?" growled Lint. "You want us to follow rats? Didn't you hear what that creature said about this 'Old Code?'"

"Yes. They said we don't have to believe in it," said York.

"They may *say* we don't have to, but you'll see. You'll see. By the end of all this, we'll either be dead," Lint jabbed his cane in the rats' direction, "or worse: living like them."

"You're being paranoid, Lint. It's just three rats," reassured Pine before heading into the grass himself. "Wall-mice and cage-mice combined, there's at least over a hundred of us. As long as we stick together, what's the worst that could happen?"

"But they're rats!" the old-timer hollered to the mice as they crossed the lawn. "You can't trust rats!"

Chapter 4

Water, Corn . . . and More Water

For the rest of the day the mice and the rats continued their journey, crossing through a small patch of trees and into a grassy plain. Other than a barbed wire fence, the rodents saw no signs of human life.

As night approached, Benny assumed the rats would stop to sleep, but still they scurried on. As the sun vanished, Benny could not see beyond the heads of the three rats he followed. The hot summer night came alive with the sounds of chirping insects, hooting owls, and barking coyotes. Sounds unfamiliar to the mice. Strange sounds. Frightening sounds.

"How can they even see where they are going?" mumbled Cookie.

"Crumb needs to rest. What are the rats expecting? To just leave the little ones behind?" Rose muttered to Humphrey.

"It would be pointless to escape the humans only to starve," agreed Pine, wiping beads of sweat from his dark brown fur.

"Why didn't we just stay in the walls of the humans' house?" asked

Cookie. "You wall-mice were fine there."

"Pib, Fib, and Tib," grumbled Lint. The ancient mouse kept in pace with the others, despite the use of a cane.

"Excuse me?"

"Pib, Fib, and Tib. See those three numbskulls?" Lint scowled in the direction of three identical mice with bright red fur, currently flirting with one of Cookie's daughters. The female mouse giggled as the mouse trio literally fought for her attention, yanking at each other's tails, biting and scratching. All three were huge, in mouse standards, twice the size of Benny. "Those three have dung for brains. They thought it was a good idea to steal from the humans' food pantry."

"And they were caught?" asked Cookie.

"No, but Mother Human didn't have to be a genius to realize it wasn't raisins in her cereal," replied Lint.

A few of the babes, and even the older mice, chuckled at this.

"You can all laugh, but Father Human talked of poison and traps . . . and even a cat," said Lint in a serious tone. "Rose spoke of your escape, so Pine figured we'd join you. Strength in numbers, eh?"

Humphrey looked adoringly at his mate. "So it was you that planned it all?"

Rose blushed. "No . . . I wouldn't say me. Mad came up with most of the plan." Her eyes wandered to the front of the line, where the three rats led the group.

"Wait," said York. "The male rat's name is Mad?"

"That's what he calls himself." said Rose. "Or, at least, I think that's how I heard his daughter address him."

Lint spat into the dirt. "Mice shouldn't be following rats. They aren't to be trusted. Rats keep too many secrets."

Humphrey leaned over as they walked and licked Rose's cheek. "At least mice don't keep secrets," he said in his quiet voice.

Rose did not reply.

Pine, the leader of the wall-mice, twitched his whiskers nervously. A twitch so slight only Benny had noticed.

The mice continued following Dolley, Mad, and Moon through the night. As the first rays broke the horizon, Benny saw they were in a ditch, traveling next to a trickling stream. Benny noticed something peculiar floating in the water. He scooped it up with a paw and examined its smooth, yellow surface.

It was a corn kernel.

Throughout the hot day, the rodents traveled on. The three rats ignored the occasional squeak of protest from the mice, complaining of weary paws or cramping hunger pains.

Just as the sun was setting, the rats froze in their tracks and the train of mice bumped into each other.

The group stood before a solid wall of cornstalks, continuing in both directions as far as the eye could see. To the right of the rodents stood a single mighty cottonwood tree. The mice had to squint just to see where the tree ended and the sky began.

None spoke. None moved, taking in the magical moment with awe and disbelief.

The rodent pilgrims had finally arrived at their destination.

The travelers, too exhausted to search for food in the field, nestled in grass near the roots of the cottonwood tree for a well-deserved night's sleep.

Except for the rats.

Instead of sleeping under the tree like the mice, the family of rats had immediately begun digging into the dirt away from the cottonwood.

Benny, curious of what the rats were about, watched their shadowy forms. From time to time, the rats would appear, panting, covered in dirt, their eyes bloodshot. Benny watched Moon roll out large pebbles, her once sleek and shiny white fur now coated with mud.

A few mice still awake shook their heads and scoffed at the rats' lunacy.

There was a soft rumble in the distance, but Benny went to sleep, dismissing the noise as nothing.

A flash of light.

An explosion.

Benny awoke, up to his whiskers in water and mud. His younger siblings squeaked with fright and dug their faces into York's side. Benny squinted his eyes as rain whipped against his face.

"What do we do, York?" shouted Cookie as his own babes clutched his tail.

York saw the mound of dirt of the rats' burrow poking above the grass. "Benny, look after your siblings," he called out and scurried in the direction of the rats' home.

York vanished down the hole and a few seconds later reappeared, cursing madly.

"What is it? Will they let us in?" Humphrey asked as York rejoined his soaked mice brethren.

"No," replied York.

"What? Why not?"

"Remember that Old Code they talked about?"

"Yes. What about it?" said Humphrey.

"They said allowing us in would 'break it.'"

"So this Old Code says to let others freeze in the rain?" asked Lint, incredulous.

"I don't know about the rest of you," shouted York over the roar of the storm, "but if this is just a sample of their Old Code, I want nothing to do with it."

There was a hearty agreement throughout the rest of the soaking wet mice; however, this did not solve the problem of the rain.

For the rest of the night, Benny was miserable. Although he was cold and shivering on the outside, inside, his gut became warm with hate and envy. What creatures were so mean to not even share a simple hole in the ground?

These same feelings could be said of the rest of the mice, whose eyes peered through the darkness at the rats' home where the selfish creatures slept, dry and warm.

The next morning, when the rain had ceased, all the mice, though sleep deprived, were busy shoveling mud with their paws, building their own burrow under the shade of the cottonwood tree.

Chapter 5

Work and Games

During midday, after a short nap, the mice's stomachs growled with hunger. The aroma of corn floated by the tips of their noses. They all ventured into the field and began searching between the cornstalks, but to their horror, they could not find even a single kernel.

"Where is it?" asked a wall-mouse. "I smell it everywhere, but I don't see it."

"Hey, over here!" York called out. He stood next to a leafy ear lying in a muddy puddle. "The corn smell is coming from this."

With great effort, York and a few other mice began to peel and chew away at the thick, leathery husk. After the long, laborious task, the golden kernels were exposed. Next, York and the others, using their teeth, tore the kernels from the cob.

Once finished, the mice gathered around a small pile of corn. "Well, it's not much," York panted, a slight frown on his face.

"Not much!" said Cookie. "That will barely feed half my family. I would have to work myself ragged until midday to collect enough to feed my own."

"And we were lucky with this one," said Pine. "How are we supposed to reach those way up there?" He pointed to the ears of corn high above their heads, jutting out from the stalks.

From behind the crowd there was a rustle of leaves.

The three rats were chewing and gnawing at the base of another cornstalk. A while later, the stalk slowly tilted forward, and the mice scurried away as it crashed into the dirt. The rats went to work, removing the ear from the stalk and, repeating the process of the mice, removing the husk, as well as the corn kernels. By the end of the process, the creatures were dripping with sweat, staring at a corn pile the same size of York's.

A brother of Benny leaned close and whispered, "I liked it better when the human just gave us food. Are we actually going to have to work every time we want to eat?"

Benny did not reply. Instead, he headed towards a stalk and, like the rats had done, began to gnaw at its base. Over time, one by one, the mice conceded to their hunger, and soon all were working to harvest the corn.

In the afternoon, the mice sat staring at their individual piles of corn, not knowing how to transport the food to their burrow. Even the rats stood, scratching the dandruff from their heads in frustration.

Benny caught sight of his sister Hazel. Too young to help harvest, she was pulling a corn leaf through the dirt like a sled while a younger babe sat on top, giggling.

This gave Benny an idea.

First, Benny tore a leaf off a fallen corn stalk. Next, he placed his corn on top of the leaf. Pulling on the leaf's edge with his mouth, Benny discovered his idea worked. With greater ease, he began dragging the corn pile towards his family's burrow back at the cottonwood tree. Seeing Benny's ingenious invention, the mice cheered and began to do the same, as well as the rats.

Once returning to their burrows, they feasted on the corn until nothing was left. Late into the evening, they sang and danced.

However, the singing and dancing grew old and repetitive. But mice babes are creative in remedying boredom, and it was not long till the young mice invented a game.

York and Cookie approached. "We heard all the laughing. What's going on here?"

The young babes, proud of their creation, happily showed the adults how to play their game.

The playing field consisted of a large circle. On the perimeter, each mouse laid a husk leaf, which would be a "burrow." The goal was to drop as much "corn," represented by pebbles, into the burrow without the corn being knocked away or stolen by another mouse.

"What do you call it?" asked Pine, fascinated.

"Burrow Rush," a babe called out.

"Can we play?" asked Cookie and York.

Soon, more adults joined the game. Before the sun set, all mice were either playing Burrow Rush or cheering from the sidelines.

The entire time, Benny had watched from a distance.

It was not long until the triplets, Fib, Tib, and Pib, began arguing for a new rule about throwing the corn at other players, and the game had to be paused.

York approached his son, panting from all the activity. "Benny, why don't you join in?"

Benny shrugged.

The crowd surrounding the Burrow Rush field burst into laughter as Fib, Tib, and Pib began to settle their differences by wrestling in the dirt. Lint attempted to break them up with the use of his cane.

"Father?"

"Yes?" York did not turn his eyes from the Burrow Rush field, caught up in the excitement.

"Why are the rats still out in the field gathering corn?"

The elder mouse peered over his shoulder just in time to see the rat, Moon, dragging her second leaf filled with corn into their burrow. A few minutes later, she appeared again, scurrying back to the cornfield.

Benny felt a twinge of guilt, as if he should be doing the same.

York patted his son on the back, shaking his head in disgust at the rats' actions.

"That, Benny, is an example of greed, which is a horrible way to live one's life."

The game of Burrow Rush continued until the sun had fully set. All the mice said their good nights and headed back to their warm burrows. Before Benny scurried down his own burrow to join his snoring siblings and father, he saw the shadows of Mad, Dolley, and Moon emerge from the field. Their paws bled, their sleek fur was scuffled in all directions, and they groaned from the strain of the weight as they pulled the leaves of corn to their burrows.

Benny pondered why the rats would put themselves through such torture. Indeed, it seemed Mad *was* mad.

That night, the mice slept with their bellies full, in cozy burrows, comforted by knowing none would be fed to a snake.

Then came the opossum.

Chapter 6

Death and Cowardice

Benny awoke to his siblings' screams.

The ground shook and the whole roof of the burrow collapsed, smothering him. Benny clawed at the earth until the cold night slapped against his face. He took in big gulps of air and pulled himself from the hole.

"Father!" he cried. "Father!"

As Benny turned around, he froze, staring at the backside of what appeared to be an enormous rodent, ten times bigger than any rat. It had white fur, a leathery tail twice as long as Benny, and a bald pink snout. The creature made a heavy panting sound as it clawed at the ground where Benny's burrow had been.

A young female mouse screamed as the creature uncovered its first prize. It was Daisy, one of Benny's sisters. Only her head was exposed. Daisy didn't even have time to blink away the dirt. The creature plucked her from the ground like a carrot, and with its sharp teeth, silenced her screams in a few chews and a swallow. The creature continued to dig, searching for more prey, following the muffled screams of the young ones.

A flame of hatred began to burn inside Benny, and all thought and reason left his mind. He charged forward, bearing his fangs, releasing a hiss.

The monster's tail slapped down next to him.

Benny was opening his mouth to bite the opossum's tail when he was suddenly jerked backwards and dragged through the dirt away from the creature.

It was Mad, his tail wrapped around Benny's throat.

"Let me go," Benny spat and hissed. He scratched at Mad's tail, leaving deep, bloody gashes.

The rat only grimaced.

As Benny was hauled into the rats' burrow, the last thing he saw was the monster snap back its head, tossing one of his brothers into the air, and then catching the pitiful thing fully in its jaws. Only the mouse's twitching whiskers protruded from the monster's fangs.

Benny toppled down into the burrow, and Mad uncoiled his tail from the mouse's neck. Benny stood up, blinded by tears. "Why don't you help them? Are you just going to let them die? Let me go! I have to stop that . . . that thing!"

Mad joined his mate and daughter huddled in the corner. Dolley looked at Benny with her one good eye and motioned for him to be quiet by placing a claw to her lips. Benny turned and rushed to the tunnel leading out of the burrow.

In a flash, Moon stood between him and the exit.

"Get out of my way!" he squeaked.

The young rat did not move, her eyes peering into Benny's as if she could not understand why he was so upset.

Benny tried to scurry around, but she was faster, and again, blocked his escape.

"Why won't you let me go!" Benny cried.

"If you go out there, you will die," Moon said calmly.

Benny snapped. He screamed and shouted, scratching madly at the dirt walls. "Father! Father! Somebody help! I need to save my family! Somebody!"

"Mouse, be quiet," Moon hissed, grabbing his tail and pulling him away from the wall.

"Father! Somebody! Help!"

"Quiet, or you'll kill us all," said Dolley.

"I don't care if I die! I don't care! I have to save my—"

Benny's world was filled with an explosion of color, and his body went limp. Before his eyes closed, he saw a small rock drop from the paw of Mad.

Darkness.

Benny's eyes fluttered open. There was a dull throbbing on the top of his skull behind his ear. He tapped the wound tenderly, feeling the hair crusted with blood. He peered around. Daylight. Outside? How had he—

He remembered.

"Father! My . . . my family," he meant to shout the words but they came out mumbled. "The beast . . . I have to get back to . . ." Benny tried to stand, but his legs lacked the strength.

"Oh my!" It was Rose. "He's awake! York, he's awake!"

York approached, his eyes bloodshot and fur filthy. "Thank our Ancestors! You're still alive," York said, falling to his knees and wrapping Benny in his arms.

"Father, did everyone else escape?"

Tears welled in York's eyes as he pointed behind Benny.

Benny turned and saw Hazel, his youngest sister, lying in the grass with a deep gash in her side. At first he thought her dead, but her chest moved with a strained breath.

"Where . . . where is everyone else?"

"They're . . . they're . . ." But the words could not find their way, and the elder mouse turned, his back heaving with sobs.

Benny knew.
Dead.

Chapter 7

The Beginning of the End

Rumors quickly spread that the decision to leave the humans was a mistake. There was talk of returning to the house and risking the traps, poison, and even a cat.

York and Pine called the cage-mice and wall-mice to a meeting at midday near the base of the cottonwood to discuss options. The six eldest mice, Rose, Pine, York, Cookie, Humphrey, and Lint, had climbed up the trunk of the tree and stood on the lowest branch, overlooking the crowd.

To everyone's surprise, even Mad and his family had ceased their labor in the fields to attend. The rats sat farthest back on a cottonwood root protruding from the ground, allowing them to peer over the heads of the mice.

"I'll just go ahead and say what's on everyone's minds," stated Pine. "Should we stay here, or should we go back to the house?"

The crowd exploded with shouts of opinions.

"Stay here! There's food!"

"No, the beast will return!"

"We can dig deeper!"

"What about the humans? We had homes, and we didn't have to work for our food!"

"You wall-mice didn't have to worry about the snake!"

"You cage-mice didn't have to scrounge for food!"

"I'm a wall-mouse, and I like living out here!"

"I'm a cage-mouse, and I like it too!"

"Well, I'm a cage-mouse, and I hate living—"

"*Buuuuuuum!*"

The crowd fell silent. Earlier that day, Lint had discovered a bottle cap in the cornfield. When hit with his cane, he had found it made a deep resounding gong.

"Thank you, Lint," said Pine.

The old mouse gave a stern nod. "Knew this thing would come in handy."

Pine turned his attention back to the crowd. "I think it can be safely said that no longer are there wall-mice and cage-mice. We are all mice. We are all one clan. At the same time, we are also individuals. We will take a vote and follow the decision of the majority. Does anyone disagree with this, and if so, please just raise your paw."

No paws were raised, not even the rats'.

"Now," said Pine, "before we decide if we should stay or go back to the humans, if there are any other ideas, please raise your paw to be called on."

For a few seconds, nothing happened. Slowly, one paw raised into the air.

It was Benny.

"Yes, Benny?" asked York gently.

"We fight the opossum."

Members of the crowd chuckled. Even Benny's father had a sympathetic smile.

"Why not? With enough volunteers, we could scare it away!"

Lint shook his head. "And who would these volunteers be? You?" He looked at the rest of the mice. "Are there any here willing to risk their lives for the good of us all?"

A few whispered, but no paws were raised.

However, Benny would not give up so easily. "What . . . what if we rewarded them?"

"Reward them? How?" asked Lint. "With death?"

Suddenly, York motioned for the five other mice to join him. He whispered a few words, to which the elders nodded in agreement, and then the group separated.

"We believe," announced York, "that a defense against the opossum would be feasible. However, it would require time for training, planning, and a vigil watch. This would allow the other mice to work and live in peace. As for payment for these services, these . . . these *defenders* will no longer have to work in the field."

An excited murmur broke out.

"But how—"

"Please raise your paw."

A paw was raised.

"Yes."

"If the defenders don't work in the field, how are they going to eat?"

More murmurs. A bang of the bottle cap gong silenced them.

"Since the defenders will be serving all mice, all mice will contribute a single kernel from each leaf harvested to a pile. This pile will then be divided and shared amongst the defenders."

"So, you're saying if we become defenders, we don't have to harvest. Instead, we will just pick up corn at a pile?"

"Yes," York replied. "However, since all harvesters are giving only one kernel, they will still have plenty left for themselves and their families. No mouse will miss one single kernel from a whole leaf filled with corn."

Excited about this new proposal, the mice whispered:

"I'd be willing to join and fight if I didn't have to work in the field."

"It'd be nice to have someone on constant guard for our protection."

"I just have to pay one kernel from a whole leaf of corn, and I will be defended? What a marvelous notion!"

Soon, the whispers broke into chatter, chatter which broke into cheers, and cheers that were joined by uproarious applause of mice slapping the ground with their tails. A paw smacked Benny's back. "Brilliant young 'un! Defending each other. Looking out for one another. Supporting each other. Exactly what it means to be a mouse!"

"So, do we have any volunteers?" York asked.

More than half the crowd raised their paws. Seeing the patriotism, there was another loud cheer.

York motioned for the crowd to settle down and stepped forward, clearing his throat. As he spoke, his eyes began to water. "Last night, I lost nearly all of my family." Benny cast his gaze to the ground, feeling his own tears form. "But now, as I look before me, I realize something: you are my family. A family with freedom. None will be able to stop our progress. But a vote must still be cast. So, if you wish to return to the humans' house, please raise your paw."

The reply was silence, no paw in sight.

"If you wish to stay here, to create a defense, to contribute, and to live. Raise! Your! Paw!"

Each mouse thrust up an arm, and there was an ear-bursting roar of approval.

Benny glanced at the rats perched on the protruding root. Their paws were also raised, but the three did not cheer.

Immediately after the gathering, a place to contribute corn for the defenders was constructed. It was made from a beer can. The artifact had been discovered by Crumb when playing in the rows of cornstalks the day before.

Several mice dragged the can to the edge of the field, closer to the burrows and sat it upright. Next, in order to create a wider opening to toss the corn into, the mice, using their strong incisors, chewed around the aluminum lid. Finally, a latch was made near the bottom of the can to allow easy access for the defenders to pull out their corn when desired.

That evening, the first defenders were chosen by the elders.

Pib, Tib, and Fib were the first picks, being the largest and strongest of the mice. Other chosen defenders were a mixture of wall-mice and cage-mice. All were larger and stronger than young Benny.

As Stud, the strong son of Pine, turned from the six elder mice and brushed past Benny, he looked down at the black mouse's trivial stature and whispered. "You, a defender? You're basically a babe. I doubt it."

Benny ignored Stud and approached the elder mice. In one glance, the elders chuckled, including Benny's father.

Lint leaned over and whispered into York's ear.

Benny's father nodded and approached Benny. He rustled the fur on his son's head playfully. "I'm proud of your commitment. Maybe in another moon or so, but for now, you work the fields."

"But I was the one who came up with the idea!"

York tapped Benny's head with his tail. "Yeah, well, then let's keep that head intact so you keep coming up with ideas."

"Father, please—"

"No, Benny. I've already lost—" York lowered his voice and scooted closer to his son. "I've already lost all your brothers and sisters. And Hazel . . . well, Rose says she doesn't look too good. She might not last through the night. So please, Benny, I can't lose you too. You're all I have left. Please, for me."

Benny wiped his eyes but gave a firm nod.

"Thank you, Son. Now, why don't you go check on your sister and keep her company. For the both of us."

Benny turned and left the cottonwood tree, patting down the black fur his father had ruffled. He winced as his paw touched the tender spot behind his ear where Mad had struck him. The wound reminded him of how the rats had cowered in their burrow, and how they had not cheered when voting for the defenders.

Benny decided rats were selfish cowards.

Chapter 8

A Deal with the Devil

Earlier that morning, before the meeting underneath the cotton-wood tree, a few volunteers helped dig a new burrow for York and his pitifully reduced family. Hazel, due to her condition, had been carried inside and placed on a fresh nest of grass.

Benny sat next to his unconscious sister and stroked her brown fur. Slowly, with a strange wheezing sound, her sides would expand with each breath. The gash on her abdomen had formed a dark red scab.

Suddenly, Benny noticed a shadow fall over her form. He turned to see Dolley and Mad standing next to him, studying his sister with intense, hungry gazes.

Benny hissed. "Get out of here. Get out!"

The rats were startled, and despite their size, began to shrink away as Benny charged them, extending his claws. "Leave her alone! If you touch her, I'll kill you! You hear me? I'll kill you!"

He scratched at the air before them again, but this time, Mad caught his wrist in his claws and pulled Benny close.

"Is she worth anything to you," Dolley growled next to her mate. Her breath smelled sour. "What about your father? Does he care for her?"

Benny glared at them. He would not be intimidated. "Everything. She is worth everything to us. Now, get—"

Before Benny could finish, in a black and white blur, the rats vanished from the burrow.

For the next four days, Hazel only grew worse. The scab began to ooze a green substance that smelled like urine. Her face lost all color and her wheezing breaths had begun to slow.

Benny, unable to watch his sister's deteriorating condition, kept himself busy by gathering corn in the field until midday. In the afternoon, he watched in fascination as the defenders trained at clawing and biting.

Pib, Tib, and Fib had an aura of leadership about them and soon took command of the defenders, having them do exercises that consisted of leaping and biting a corn cob, as well as climbing to the top of the cottonwood tree hauling a leaf full of stones.

When taking a break from these exercises, the defenders would file their claws on stones, sharpening them to such a point that they could slash through bark as though it were made of mud.

Each day, after Benny and his father had finished harvesting, they stopped by the empty beer can to contribute to the pile for the defenders.

York would grab a kernel off both their leaves and toss them over the edge of the can with a loud *klink*. "Just think, Benny, with just those two corn kernels, we are helping everyone stay safe."

Benny slept soundly under the constant gaze of the defenders . . . or maybe it was because the rats hadn't been seen since sneaking into Benny's burrow.

Some believed the rats had missed the pampering of Younger

Brother Human and had scampered back to the human's house in regret.

Benny hoped this was true. Even better, he hoped the humans had killed them.

More days passed, and Hazel began to vomit.

Lint confronted York. The two scooted away from Benny, but the young black mouse was able to overhear the two elders' whispers.

"I've seen this before, York. Hazel is dying from a strange sickness of the wound. It's not healing. She's in pain, and I'd be surprised if she gets through tonight."

"No, you're wrong. She just needs more—"

"York, be sensible."

There was a pause.

"What should I do?" the father pleaded.

"Well, the last time I saw this, the wall-mouse was in complete misery for hours before his death, puking and peeing all over itself. It begged for its life to just end."

"What are you suggesting? That I kill my only daughter?"

"We could get Pib, Fib, or Tib in here to do it. You and Benny could wait outside. It would be—"

"No! I . . . I won't do it! I . . . I can't."

Lint placed a paw on York's shoulder. "Look at her. She's suffering, York. Suffering. Would a loving father wish that on his daughter?"

There was silence.

York glanced at Hazel. "Will . . . will it be quick?"

Benny couldn't believe what he was hearing.

"Better than this, York. Better than this."

As the two turned to leave the burrow, they stopped in their tracks.

Blocking their way stood Mad and his one-eyed mate, Dolley. Both of the rats' faces were ragged. Their eyes bloodshot with deep shadows. Through their fur, the ridges of ribs could be seen, evidence that they had lost weight. The creatures smelled as though they had not rinsed in a stream for days.

Mad held a piece of torn tissue paper in one paw. In the other, he held what appeared to be a pure white pebble, smooth all over except for one side, which was chipped and jagged. There was something carved into the smooth side in strange symbols.

Benny stepped forward, ready to defend his sister, but York placed a paw on his son's chest and asked Mad, "What do you want?"

Dolley answered. "Your son told us your daughter was worth everything to you. Is this true?"

"Don't talk to them, York," spoke up Lint, but York raised his other paw, silencing him as well.

"Yes, that is true. Why?"

"We have learned how to save her," said Dolley. "However," the rat added, noticing a spark of hope in York's eyes, "my mate desires a trade."

"What do you want?"

"A full leaf of corn," Dolley replied.

"Are you insane? I would be out in the field working twice—"

"I wasn't finished!" Dolley hissed. "A leaf of corn every day until the next full moon."

Benny's jaw dropped.

"The next full moon!" shouted York. "That would be over fifteen leaves of corn."

Dolley nodded. "We know."

"You cold-hearted rodent. Why won't you just help her?" asked York. "Why won't you just do the kind and decent thing?"

Mad turned to leave.

"He'll take that as a no," said a slightly amused Dolley.

"Wait!" York cried. His whiskers drooped in defeat. "You'll get your corn. Just save my babe."

"Happily," Dolley purred. The rat turned her head to the opening of the burrow. "They agreed, Moon! Get down here with that water and soap!"

Soap? What's soap? Benny wondered.

Dolley turned back to the mice. "Now, if you would please excuse us, we need to work in peace."

"But she's my sister!" said Benny. "I need to be here for her."

"Do not worry, young mouse," spoke Mad, his black eyes staring at Benny. "We will do our best. Our corn depends on it."

York placed a paw on Benny's back and pushed him towards the exit. "Let's go, Benny. We don't have a choice."

As Benny, Lint, and York left the burrow, Moon scurried past. The young rat held a thimble of water and a broken chunk of a white, waxy substance Benny assumed was soap.

The three mice sat outside the hole, and hours passed. Soon, the sun began to set. Word spread of York's deal with the rats, and a crowd formed around the entrance of the burrow. Occasionally, Moon would appear, clutching bloody tissue paper, running into the darkness of the night, and then returning with either water, more tissue, thread, or a chunk of soap.

Realizing the rats would be working through the night, many mice returned back to their homes, muttering how greedy the rats were to take advantage of a mouse with a dying daughter.

Lint stood up, shaking his head, "You shouldn't have accepted their offer, York. Never trust rats. Never." With that, the old-timer hobbled off.

The next morning, Benny and York awoke to the sound of Hazel crying.

The two rushed down into the burrow. The gash on her side was now clean and sewn with thread. The blood, vomit, and mud was washed from Hazel's fur. Next to her sat a few corn kernels for a meal and a leaf holding a pool of drinking water.

The rats were gone.

Chapter 9

Sweaty Miracles

At midday, while mice left the field, dragging leaves of corn behind them, Benny and his father continued to labor on to pay off their debt to Mad. It was not until late into the afternoon, after their paws felt ready to fall off, they had their second leaf.

The two stopped by the beer can to contribute. Benny threw in a kernel and began to pull his leaf.

His father stopped him. "A kernel for every leaf, Benny. We filled two leaves, so you must throw in a second kernel."

"Why? We worked our tails off for that second leaf. None of the other mice filled a second leaf."

"Benny, all the mice agreed. We must do what our society deems necessary."

"Well, if we start contributing the most, do you think the defenders will protect us more than the other mice?"

"Benny!" York snapped. "What a selfish thought! The defenders protect all mice equally. Now throw your corn in!"

Benny did as he was told.

That night, Dolley came to check on Hazel. Besides whimpering in fear while the large one-eyed white rat poked and prodded her, Hazel was doing quite well.

Dolley turned to them. "Corn."

York frowned and nodded to the leaf in the corner of the burrow.

Without a word, the one-eyed rat snatched the corn and left.

Benny and York continued to work late into the afternoon, unable to join the others in songs, dances, and games. However, the two were never alone, for the rats would harvest into the evening unless approached by a mouse in need of medical attention.

The miracle of Hazel's recovery was now known to all. The rats were more than willing to help . . . for a price. For a young mouse who had sliced his paw on a sharp stone, they charged one full leaf. Stud, the strong son of Pine, broke his tail when climbing down the cottonwood after lookout duty. They tied his tail firmly to a straight stick and charged him four leaves of corn.

Although each mouse grumbled at the high costs, the rats did their jobs well. The young mouse's paw healed cleanly, and even Stud, after a few days, claimed his tail, though still strapped to a stick, felt as good as new.

Hearing stories of the amazing recoveries prompted mice to harvest a few extra kernels each day, saving a stash to pay the rats in case any harm ever befell them or their loved ones.

Lint, the feeble old mouse, would shake his head and laugh. "You're all acting like a bunch of paranoid fools! I would never give the rats that much corn!"

"But what if something happened to you?" asked Benny.

"Ha! I've lived three of your lifetimes," Lint said, jabbing Benny in the stomach with his cane, "and I've never gotten sick. What do I have to worry about?"

Chapter 10

The Generosity of Generocity

One day, Rose and Humphrey called for a meeting underneath the cottonwood tree. The motherly female stood and talked. "As you all know, while Cookie and York work in the field, I watch over their babes, as well as my own. However, I have discussed an idea with the elder mice: why not watch over *all* the babes who have yet to see their eighth moon?"

There was an excited murmur. Benny perked up his ears. Although he was on his tenth moon, Hazel had only just seen her third full moon. (Thank goodness, because it signaled they were finished with their payments to Mad.)

After quieting the mice, Rose continued. "Since I would be too busy to harvest, all I ask is to receive enough corn from the Kindness Pile every day to feed myself."

"The 'Kindness Pile?'" mice whispered, confused.

Pine stood and explained. "We felt *Kindness Pile* was an appropriate name, as it is kindness that causes us to look after one another."

The mice slapped their tails against the ground, politely applauding the clever title.

The rats did not.

Pib raised his paw, and the elders called on him. "If she will be getting corn from the Kindness Pile, will there be enough food for us, the defenders?"

"Ah, yes," said Cookie. "I have been counting the corn. We merely need to contribute two kernels per leaf instead of one."

Seeing hesitant looks, Rose stepped in. "But think about it: with just one more piece of corn, you won't have to worry about your babes for half the day. Not only that, but I will love them, just like they were my own. I will teach them about our history with the humans, how the Kindness Pile works, how to harvest grain, the names of objects, and even how to count. This way, they will grow to be productive members of this society."

What a marvelous idea, all the mice thought.

"I'm not sending my babes!"

The statement came from Dolley, her one eye ablaze.

Lint hobbled forward, looking down at Dolley from the branch and smacked his gums. "Don't be daft! Moon is too. . ." But his voice trailed off, taking notice of the rat's enlarged stomach. "Oh, I see," he muttered. As did everyone else.

Dolley was pregnant.

"Now, now, Dolley," said Humphrey, coming to the defense of his mate. "I can assure you my Rose is a loving, wonderful mouse who would take good care of your babes."

"I do not doubt that," replied Dolley, "but they are my babes, and I wish to raise them. To teach them what I have learned."

"Like this 'Old Code,'" Humphrey said, rolling his eyes.

"Does it matter?" Dolley snapped back. "Am I not free to raise my babes?"

York stepped in. "If that is what you wish, then you do not have to send your babes to Rose. They are yours, and as promised, all mice here are free to do as they please."

A few mice shouted in agreement with this last statement.

"However," York continued, "as Lint said before, if the vote passes, all will need to contribute."

"But my babes will be under my care," said Dolley. "Why should I still have to contribute extra kernels?"

"Because this is a place of generosity," said York. "Not all babes are as fortunate as yours, Dolley, to have a mother." It was obvious that York was referring to his own family. "In fact," York continued, "I think it is about time we gave our city a name."

"Like what?" came a shout.

"Why, how about 'Generocity?'"

All the mice, including Benny, cheered. What a clever title!

"Very well, then it is agreed: from now on, we are all proud citizens of Generocity!"

Another cheer.

Rose cleared her throat, and York whacked his own head with an open paw. "Why twist my tail! How could I forget? If you wish for Rose to start a . . ." York paused and glanced at Rose. "I'm sorry, what are you going to call this place where you will care for the babes?"

"I would call it CLAS."

"CLAS?"

"Yes: Center of Love and Schooling."

"Marvelous! If you wish for Rose to start a CLAS, then raise your paw!"

Chapter 11

Whispers and Wheezing

A little north of the cottonwood tree, if a mouse was to follow the edge of the cornfield, protruded a cinderblock from the top of a grassy knoll. The strange stone's original purpose was a mystery to the mice, yet the cinderblock made a perfect marker for designating the CLAS area.

The next morning, before heading to work in the cornfield, Benny led his fully healed sister by the paw to the cinderblock. Hazel, nervous at the change, walked quietly at her brother's side.

As the two drew closer, Hazel's ears perked up. Small mice darted around the cinderblock, emitting joyous squeaks and peals of laughter. Hazel shot off to join them, leaving Benny in the dust.

New to the experience, Benny did not know what to do next. Should he go? Was that it? He looked around and caught sight of Rose and Pine in a hushed discussion. They were unaware as Benny approached.

"... longer till he will start to notice?"

"Maybe a week."

"Do you think Humphrey will suspect? Maybe he will think they are his?"

Rose gazed at the ground. "We haven't . . . not since the night before I escaped the humans."

Pine slapped his tail against the ground and cursed out loud, "Droppings!"

"It's okay. We can finally tell him," Rose said. "I'm sure he'll understand. Then we can be—oh. Hello, Benny."

Pine stared at Benny, his eyes wide. "How long have you been standing there?"

"Is everything okay?" Benny asked.

Pine gave a weak smile. "Yes . . . yes everything is fine. I'm just helping Rose with . . . with thinking of a gift for her mate. Um, I'll see you later, Rose." The brown mouse turned and scampered off.

"Do I just leave Hazel here?"

"Oh . . . oh, yes. Just be back here a little after midday to pick her up."

As Benny headed back to the field, he noticed a group of mice standing around Lint's burrow.

"I tell you, I saw blood."

"When he coughed yesterday? I thought he said it was just a cold?"

"What's 'a cold?'"

"I don't know, but I doubt it's that."

"Has Lint asked for the help of the rats?"

"Yeah. He practically begged, but they said, 'No corn, no medicine.'"

"Why, those coldhearted furbags! Couldn't he pay them afterwards, like what York did for Hazel?"

"That's what Lint offered, but the rats said he would still be too weak to earn the corn."

"I tell you what, I'm going to start saving even more corn. I don't want to end up like Lint. I don't know what I'd do if something like this happened to me or my babes."

"Well, if it were me, and I knew how to heal, I'd do it for free . . ."

The conversation faded as Benny walked past and into the field.

Later, as Benny sweated and toiled, he thought back to what the mice had said of the rats, and of all the corn the rats received for healing the sick.

He could do the same. It didn't look hard, and if he charged less than the rats, he would steal all their business and still make more than what he harvested in the field. Plus, he would be helping others. If they couldn't pay, like Lint, he would still heal them.

It would be the generous thing to do.

Suddenly, Benny had an idea.

Chapter 12

Where Is the Pity?

"He . . . hello?" Benny called down the entrance of the burrow. No reply.

Maybe they weren't home?

"What do you want?"

Benny swirled around to see Moon with a leaf full of corn behind her. She was panting and covered with sweat.

"I was wanting to speak with your father."

"Are you wanting to learn The Old Code? You'd be the first."

Benny shook his head. "Healing."

"Well, he's not here," she muttered. "Besides, you look fine to me."

"I don't need to be healed. I was just wondering if . . . well . . . do you think he would teach me how to heal others?"

Moon gave a snort, grabbed the stem of her leaf, and dragged the corn into the burrow, disappearing from sight.

Benny called down into the hole, but she did not answer.

Fed up, Benny stormed off.

The next day, while in the field, Moon approached Benny.

"I told my father what you asked. He said 'No.'"

Benny's heart dropped.

"But," the white rat added, "I also told him how hard I've seen you work. How you're different than the rest. He's going to give you one chance. My father says bring half a leaf of corn or don't bother coming at all."

Moon left.

"Thank you!" Benny called out, but the white rat didn't look back. The conversation was over.

As usual, the mice stopped their work at midday, each dragging one leaf of corn, happily saying to one another, "Can you believe it? We just have to work in the field for a few hours, deposit two kernels, and we don't have to worry about defending ourselves or taking care of our babes till midday!"

"Yeah, I just wish I didn't have to walk them all the way to CLAS," one mouse grumbled.

"I don't mind it."

"That's because your burrow is closest to the cinderblock."

"Maybe you should talk to the elder mice? I'd bet they would have an idea."

Once they left, Benny worked in silence. Though he had filled one leaf, he had to earn another half a leaf to bring to Mad for later that evening.

While taking a break, he noticed a figure rushing back and forth in the stalks farther off in the field. It was Moon. She worked at a furious pace, gnawing at the stalks, tearing off the husks, and ripping off the kernels.

Benny shook his head and went back to his work, muttering, "Is she trying to kill herself? You'd think there wasn't enough food." But as the afternoon continued on, Benny found himself repeatedly glancing back at the young rat.

At one point, Moon caught one of his stares, and the two froze. Benny blushed in embarrassment and went back to work.

Later, as Benny left the field, he saw Moon was already ahead of him. She had tied the stems of three leaves, heaped full of corn, and was dragging them to the Kindness Pile. There, she took two kernels from each leaf, totaling six kernels, and threw them into the beer can.

Dolley also approached. She dragged six leaves, payments from the mice they had healed. Six!

Dolley tossed twelve kernels into the Kindness Pile, and the two rats slunk home, dragging their loads.

When Benny returned to Generocity, the mice were already feasting on corn, singing, dancing, and playing rounds of Burrow Rush.

Benny found his father next to Pine and Cookie, cheering on the Burrow Rush players from the sideline.

After telling them what he had just witnessed, the three mice completely lost interest in the game.

"Six leaves! Are you sure?" York asked. "With that much corn, you'd think they would share it."

"It makes me wonder why they don't help Lint," said Pine. "It's not like they need the corn. They have plenty."

Cookie snorted. "Guess rats really are that greedy."

"Agreed!" Pine and York said in unison.

"It's too bad we can't *force* them to help Lint. The old mouse will probably be dead by the end of the week."

York nibbled on a corn crumb and watched Hazel play tag in the distance. "Yes. Too bad," he muttered. York then shook his head, as if awakening himself from a dream and turned his attention to Benny. "Well, are you going to go play with the other mice?"

"No, I'm going to . . . to be busy for the rest of the night."

"Really? With what?" York peered over Benny's shoulder at the leaf filled with corn behind his son. "And what are you doing with that half a leaf of corn? Our burrow is the other way."

Benny told his father about the deal he had made with Mad.

"But the rat wants half a leaf of corn!" exclaimed Cookie. "York you need to talk with those creatures. They are taking advantage of your son."

York looked down at Benny, "Are you sure about this?"

Benny nodded.

"Well, okay. Just be safe."

As Benny walked away, he heard Cookie mutter, "I'd like to learn how to heal, too . . . but for half a leaf? Droppings! What fool would pay that much to learn? What would be the point?"

Chapter 13

Complications

$\mathbf{M}$oon was standing outside the burrow. "Do you have your leaf? Good. Follow me." She went down the hole.

Benny hesitated, thinking back to Cookie's comment. Was this a crazy idea? Maybe he should leave. How could he trust them?

Moon poked out her head. "Well, come on, Mouse."

Benny went down into the burrow.

The rats had dug out more dirt, expanding their home since the night of the opossum. Dolley was on her side. She was breathing rapidly, her one eye moving wildly about. Mad stood beside his mate, a paw on her belly, his back to Benny.

"Come here, Mouse, and bring me that needle and piece of glass," Mad demanded, pointing to a corner filled with all sorts of knick-knacks. "And be quick about it!"

In the corner was thread, orange-hued bottles holding smooth rocks like what had been given to Hazel, bandages, tubes, and, most astounding of all, a pile of pages as tall as Benny, ripped from books. The pages were folded neatly, with a rock placed on top as a paper weight.

"Where's that needle and glass?" Mad called again, growing impatient.

Benny grabbed the sewing needle leaning against the dirt wall, but as he picked up the glass shard, he yipped in pain, dropped it, and licked the blood from his palm.

"Careful, Mouse. It's sharp! What did you think the cloth handle was for?"

Grabbing the shard carefully, Benny brought the two items over to Mad.

"Moon, I need the pero . . . the perox—oh, what did the humans call it? Just bring me the stuff in the brown bottle." Mad grabbed the needle and glass shard from Benny and spoke without turning his attention from Dolley. "I take it my daughter collected the corn as we agreed?"

Benny nodded.

"Good," Mad replied.

Dolley released a squeak of pain.

"What's wrong with her?" Benny asked, staring at Dolley.

"By The Old Code! Haven't you ever seen a birth?"

"Birth!" What had he gotten himself into? "Well, yeah, when Radish had her babes, but what do you need those for?" Benny asked, gesturing to the shard of glass and needle in Mad's paws.

Moon rushed over and handed her father a white cap filled with a strange smelling clear liquid.

Mad doused his paws, as well as the glass shard and needle. "Dolley should have given birth by now. They're stuck."

The rat flung off the liquid from his paws and tools and glanced at a torn picture next to him of the anatomy of a rat. "Moon, the stick."

The daughter placed a broken twig in her mother's mouth.

"Stuck? Who is . . ." and then Benny realized what Mad was about to do. "Oh droppings, you can't be serious."

Mad, sweat dripping off the tip of his snout, looked at Benny. The rat gave him a weak smile. "I guess you'll learn your half a leaf's worth tonight."

Before Benny could respond, Mad brought down the shard of glass into his mate's belly.

Blood. Lots of blood.

A few seconds later, Mad shouted, "Male," then placed a squirming, hairless rat pup into Benny's paws. "Go lay it over there in the cloth."

Benny did as he was told. No sooner had he set the creature down when Mad yelled out, "Female! Come get this one!"

Benny and Mad repeated this process several more times.

"Male!"

"Male!"

"Female!"

"Ma—" The word died in his throat. The pup did not squirm. Mad paused, but only for a second, before handing Benny the limp body. Benny stared down at the pup's unmoving form. "This is no time for sorrow!" the rat hissed, his forepaws deep inside his mate's abdomen.

Benny set the dead pup down, away from the other babes, and then returned just as Mad shouted for the last time: "Male!"

Mad went through the process of sewing up the belly, sticking the needle in and out of the flesh, dragging the thread through.

Moon sifted through the objects in the corner, "I can't find the gauze!"

Mad handed the needle to Benny. Like everything else, the metal was slick with blood. "Finish it," the rat said. "Then I'll show you how to tie it off."

Benny looked at the stitching. "Right . . . right now?" he asked, but Mad was already off, busy helping his daughter.

His paws trembling, Benny stepped in front of Dolley. He was surprised how much pressure was required to push the needle into the two flaps of skin. After he pulled the thread through, and seeing Dolley still alive, Benny found the next few stitches easier to perform. As Benny stepped back to admire his work, he bumped into Mad, who had watched Benny perform the last stitch.

"Not bad," the rat said. "Not good. But not bad."

Mad took over and finished tying the knot of the stitching. Then, with Moon and Benny's help, he wrapped the lower portion of Dolley's stomach with the white gauze and carried over the six pups to nurse.

Mad whispered to his weary mate, coming up with names for the babes. At one point, he brought over the dead male. Dolley gave it a caring lick. "His name was Ceasar. Be at peace with the Ancients, young one."

Neither rat cried.

Moon showed Benny how to clean the tools using the same liquid Mad had cleaned his paws with prior to the surgery. Once all the tools were cleaned, Benny told Mad, "Well, I think I should be getting home."

"Home?" Mad peered at Benny. "Who said you were done?" The rat walked to the pile of folded papers held down with a rock. He skimmed through them until he produced a pamphlet with pictures of humans and strange symbols.

"These are instructions on performing what the humans call 'first aid.'"

"What do I do with it?" asked Benny.

"Why, you read it, and then you . . ."The rat saw Benny's eyes glaze over the confusing symbols. Mad sighed. "Well, I guess we can't all be fortunate to have our cages lined with newspaper. Moon will have to teach you how to read. From now on, bring a full leaf of corn."

"*A full leaf?*"

"In order for you to be able to learn how to heal, you must first learn how to read. It will take twice as much time, so yes, bring twice as much corn."

Benny thought back to when he had gathered corn to pay off the debt for Hazel's care. He remembered the aches, the exhaustion, and the sweat.

He was about to tell Mad where he could shove his full leaf of corn when, in the background, Moon, who was retrieving food for her mother, pulled aside a leaf acting as a makeshift curtain and revealed a large chamber full of corn. Enough corn to feed Benny for a lifetime.

"Fine," Benny muttered. "A full leaf."

Chapter 14

The Stranger from the Field

Benny trudged home.

The moon shone brightly, and the crickets played their tunes.

Long ago, the other mice had fallen asleep in their burrows. It occurred to Benny that in a few hours he would be awake again, working in the fields and heading straight back to the rats' burrow.

Was learning to heal worth it? What about his free time? What about enjoying the afternoon?

Benny thought of the mountains of corn.

The cornstalks to Benny's left rustled. He froze.

A pair of eyes reflecting the moonlight stared out at him. Slowly, the eyes grew larger as the creature approached.

It was a mouse . . . but not like any of the mice in Generocity. He was tall with abnormally large feet, and had a brown coat and a white belly.

"Hello," Benny said nervously. "What's . . . what's your name?"

The mouse pointed to himself and gave a squeak, but none of the words made sense. The mouse then pointed to the cornfield and squeaked some more, but it was all gibberish.

Benny tried to stop him. "Hold . . . hold on. Stop. I can't . . . I can't understand you."

The other mouse tilted its head, just as confused by Benny's language.

"Hey, what's going on down there?" shouted Tib from the cottonwood.

Benny looked up. "I just met this fella, but I don't think—"

"What fella?"

Benny turned and saw the strange white-bellied mouse had vanished

Chapter 15

Cruelty and Kindness

It was morning. Benny had slept in. When he exited his burrow, he was surprised to see everyone gathered underneath the cottonwood tree instead of working in the cornfield. As Benny drew near, York stood on the lower branch and was speaking down to the mice of Generocity.

"Compassion, kindness, and equality—this is what separates us from the humans. Do you agree?"

The crowd thumped their tails into the dirt in applause.

"So, it is agreed all mice have a duty to take care of their own!"

Again, more tail thumping.

"No longer shall a mouse, who has befallen injury, have to work to death to pay a medical fee. From now on a mouse may take what is demanded by the rats from the Kindness Pile."

There was a hearty agreement.

"Will Lint be able to work once he is healed?" a mouse called out.

"Ah, that brings me to the next issue. What kind of society are we if we do not take care of the elderly? So, any mouse past thirty-six moons will be able to pull a leaf of corn a day from the Kindness Pile and never have to worry about working in the field again."

The crowd cheered.

"And what about those who receive an injury, or born with a deformity?" York asked. "Should we let them starve as well?"

"Let them pull from the Kindness Pile as well!" A mouse shouted.

Tails whacked against the ground again.

"Now, in a moment, we will take a vote. But first, I will allow Rose to present the next issue."

As York backed up on the branch, Rose took his place. She was greeted by polite applause.

The CLAS teacher cleared her throat. "As you may know, there are some who live farther from CLAS than others. They have to wake up earlier and walk their babes to CLAS before heading into the field. This is time consuming and a burden. Therefore, I propose the creation of a new position. A position in which a mouse goes from burrow to burrow, collecting the babes, and walking them to CLAS. This would save parents time and provide a protective transport for each babe. However, since this mouse would be busy walking the babes, he or she should be allowed to pull a full leaf of corn from the Kindness Pile every day. For this to happen, all that is needed is for an extra kernel to be contributed from each full leaf of corn."

Again, there was polite applause.

Benny joined in. He was so busy working in the field, it would be nice to not have to worry about the chore of dropping his sister off by the cinderblock. What a great idea!

"What a bunch of stupid ideas!"

There was a gasp, and all heads swiveled. The comment had come from Moon. She was perched upon the usual root that protruded from the ground. Next to Moon was her father. Dolley was absent.

"Excuse me," said Rose, blinking her eyes in disbelief at Moon's rudeness.

"You heard me," growled Moon. "It's a bunch of stupid ideas. All of it. The transportation, the idea of providing for the old, of taking care of the sick. It's all stupid."

Rose could barely find her words. "You little . . . young rat, I understand that you have worked hard for your corn, like the rest of us, but surely you have some sympathy for the babes, as well as the sick and the old."

"No."

Rose clenched her fist. "Why you greedy, horrible—"

York stepped next to Rose and placed a paw on her shoulder and called down to the rat very calmly, "Then please tell me, Moon, what we should do about Lint and his illness, as well as the old and disabled?"

Moon gave a snort. "Let the fools die."

All the mice gasped, and there arose a grumbling.

"And of the babes who live far from CLAS?"

"That was their choice! I don't see parents' paws falling off from . . ." The last portion of Moon's sentence was overwhelmed by booing from the crowd.

"Peace! Peace!" York called out.

Moon began hissing at the mice.

The two defenders, Tib and Fib, began making their way through the crowd towards the two rats.

Mad remained expressionless through the whole ordeal.

Why wouldn't the black rat say anything? Benny wondered.

A loud bang from the gong silenced the crowd and stopped the defenders in their tracks.

"I'm sorry, Moon," York said. "I don't know how rats treat each other, but we mice wouldn't allow that. I see your mother is absent. I hear you are the sister of seven healthy—"

"Six," Moon corrected coldly.

Even Mad winced.

"Ah. Six. Well, as a sister of six, surely you are concerned for your siblings' wellbeing? What if something were to happen to your father?

Does it not provide you some comfort that they would receive a free education? What if an accident befell your brothers and sisters, and they were unable to gather corn? Does it not comfort you that they would be fed?"

"They would still be fed," replied Moon.

Mice rolled their eyes and whispered. A few chuckled.

However, Benny did not. He remembered the room full of corn in the rats' burrow.

"Why don't you put it to a vote?" Moon suggested. She looked to the crowd. "For those of you who wish to take care of yourselves and be free to decide how your corn is spent, raise a paw." At this, she raised a paw.

Only her father joined her.

More chuckles. Benny did not join in.

"Now," countered York from the branch, "If you wish to allow the old, feeble, and sick to pull from the Kindness Pile, raise your paw."

All paws of the mice were raised, even Benny's.

Benny caught Moon's stare, and he cast his eyes to the ground.

"And if you wish a mouse be hired to walk the babes to CLAS?"

Again, all mouse paws were raised.

"Any against?"

Instead of raising their paws, Mad whispered something to his daughter, and the two turned and headed back into the cornfield to work.

"The vote is passed!"

Chapter 16

A Little Here, a Lot There

Benny was drenched in sweat as he pulled the two leaves towards the Kindness Pile where Moon and Cookie were snout-to-snout in a heated argument. Mad stood quietly behind his daughter. Two defender mice stood on each side of Cookie.

"I can contribute to the Kindness Pile myself," growled Moon.

"Not anymore," replied Cookie, jabbing a thumb at his own chest. "Being one of the few mice who can count past ten, it's my job now."

"It's your job now? Counting? That's it? What about harvesting corn? How do you eat?"

"I get paid from the Kindness Pile."

"What? Did the other mice vote on this as well?" asked Moon. She looked to her father for support, but he only stood silently.

"No need," said Cookie. "The elders understood it was necessary. With the new changes, someone has to keep track of the corn going in and out of the pile."

"We wouldn't need to keep track if we didn't have this stupid pile. If we could just keep our own corn—"

"That's enough!" snapped Cookie at the young rat.

The two defenders flexed their claws.

"None of the other mice complained," said Cookie. "Why just you, Rat? Hmm? Is it because you aren't contributing like you should? Is it because you've been pulling kernels from the can when no one is looking? Is that it? Are you just nervous now because mice want to keep track?"

"You think we're stealing?" Moon lost it. "We saved you, and this is how you treat us! We should have just left you with the humans. We should have just—"

"How much?" Mad asked calmly. He gave his daughter a look of warning to stay silent.

"Excuse me?"

"How much do I have to contribute because of the changes?"

"Ten."

"Ten kernels!" Moon shouted, eyes bulging. Mad showed no response.

"You didn't let me finish. Ten kernels a leaf."

"A leaf! I filled three leaves," Moon said. "That's thirty pieces of corn from me! A full leaf of corn is—"

"—Usually fifty kernels. I know. I told you I can count. But come, now. Come, now. With how much you bring in from the field and what you charge for your healing, you rats will hardly notice a difference."

"Do it," Mad muttered, then stepped back as the three mice approached his and Moon's leaves of corn. Cookie silently counted to himself as he tossed kernel after kernel into the topless beer can, each landing with a *klink*. At each *klink*, Moon flinched as if being whipped. Mad watched, emotionless.

When finished, even Benny knew Cookie was wrong: the piles of corn on each leaf *were* noticeably smaller.

The rats grabbed their leaves and departed. Mad said nothing, but Benny heard Moon grumbling underneath her breath.

Cookie looked at Benny, and his frown turned to a smile. "Ah, Benny! Good to see you! Just like you heard: ten kernels."

Benny pushed forward one of his two leaves.

"Both of them, Benny."

"But the other leaf is to pay the rats for my education. I wouldn't have even harvested the corn if—"

"Doesn't matter," said Cookie. "Every leaf of corn is deducted. Every. Leaf."

Benny opened his mouth, but it was pointless, for Cookie was already pulling kernels from Benny's leaf and tossing them into the beer can.

"Leave," Moon said as Benny entered the rats' burrow.

"What? I brought in a whole leaf like we agreed to."

The rat pointed a claw at the leaf Benny had dragged in. "*That* is not what my father agreed to. He wants a full leaf."

"It . . . it's not my fault. I had to contribute the rest to the Kindness Pile."

"Either a full leaf, or we stop teaching."

Benny clinched his fist, considering whether to call it quits. What was he thinking? He could be outside right now, playing and having fun like the rest of the mice. Why waste his time here?

Behind Moon, the golden mountain of corn shone . . .

Chapter 17

Humphrey's Friendly Greeting

The sky burned like fire as the sun faded in the distance. As Benny trudged back to Mad's burrow with ten more kernels, he passed a few mice laughing and stumbling over one another, songs still in their throats from the day's festivities. They cast Benny curious glances as he headed into the rats' den.

As Moon collected Benny's corn, Mad began drawing pictures in the dirt and explaining something to him called "germs."

Later that evening, in the middle of a lesson about how to use soap, Cookie entered the burrow with Pib and Tib at his sides.

"What's that for?" asked Moon, nodding to a leaf of corn Tib dragged.

"For Lint's treatment, of course. As mentioned at the gathering this morning, his payments will come from the Kindness Pile."

Moon looked to her father, and the rat gave a silent nod before going back to scratching in the dirt with a claw.

Moon pointed to a corner of the burrow. "Leave it there."

"What about Lint?"

"My daughter and Benny will see to the old mouse," Mad replied without looking up.

The defenders placed the corn in the corner and the three left the burrow.

"We'll learn more about soap later," Mad said to Benny.

Moon pointed to the supply pile. "Grab those pills over there, Mouse. No, not that. The things that look like white rocks. Alright, let's get this over with."

The elderly mouse lay in his nest, almost on the point of death. With each breath Lint took came a wheezing sound. The "white rock" Benny had grabbed was the same he had seen the night Hazel had been healed.

Moon plucked the white rock from Benny's paws. "This strange stone is called 'an antibiotic,' Mouse," Moon said to Benny. "It is what kills bacteria. Things that are like germs. Hear that wheezing sound as he breathes? It's because his lungs are infected. The human that owned me had it once. Now, pay attention, because this is important: since we are so much smaller than the humans, we only need a little of the pill. Too much can kill us."

"When do I get to learn how to give anti . . . whatever?" asked Benny.

"Antibiotics." The rat broke a chunk off the pill. "That's for my father to decide. He almost died getting these from the humans, along with everything else. I'm not about to let you waste them due to your inexperience." Moon mixed the chunk with some water and poured it into Lint's mouth. The old mouse coughed and opened his eyes. Upon seeing Moon, Lint smiled. "I knew your father wasn't . . . wasn't cruel enough to . . . to let an old mouse . . . die."

The rat frowned. "I don't care if you die or not, as long as we get our corn."

The heartless words were unheard, for the old mouse was already back asleep.

"Come, Mouse," said Moon. "We might as well make a few more stops."

Next was Stud, the son of Pine. The defender was in his burrow, munching on corn taken from the Kindness Pile. Pib and Tib were also there visiting their injured fellow defender. Moon removed the stick from Stud's tail.

"Wiggle it."

The mouse did, but grimaced. "It still—ow! It still hurts."

Moon shrugged. "It's just tender. The pain will go away. I doubt you'll ever gain full movement. Still, it would have healed crooked if it hadn't been strapped straight."

"Can I still defend?" Stud asked Pib and Tib.

"We need you in peak condition in case the opossum returns," said Pib. "With your tail all stiff like that it will—"

"—It will throw off your balance," finished the rat. "You can do basic things, but climbing tall trees and fending off opossums are no longer options."

"You mean I'll have to go back to working in the field?" Stud said, horrified.

When the two finished making their rounds, they headed back to the burrow. Benny continued his reading lessons with Moon. As she drew letters in the dirt with her claws and had Benny recite the words, besides rolling her eyes at his mistakes, she was surprisingly patient. Mad stood in a corner, going through his medical supplies and flipping through human papers.

As the night before, it was late when Benny left the rats' burrow, his body aching from working in the field, and his brain on fire from all the learning.

This night, though, Benny kept his eyes peeled to the cornfield, expecting any minute to see the strange-looking, white-bellied mouse. In doing so, he bumped into Pine.

"Excuse me, young 'un . . . why, Benny! What are you doing up so late?"

"I was learning how to heal from the rats."

"Still?"

"Yes, but now I have to work even harder because I have to contribute more to the Kindness Pile."

"Hmm, well I wouldn't go blaming it on the Kindness Pile. It's those rats. They are just taking advantage of you. An education like that should be cheaper. Even free. It might be something you want—"

There was a sudden rustle in the grass a little ways off.

"Who's there?" called out Pine.

Benny wondered if it was the white-bellied mouse.

A shadowy figure approached.

"Rose, is that you? Rose?" asked Pine. "I've been waiting forever."

It was not the white-bellied mouse, and it was not Rose.

"Oh. Hello, Humphrey. I was just talking to Benny about—"

Pine was unable to finish the statement, for Humphrey had stepped right up to Pine and torn a chunk from Pine's throat with his fangs. The words turned to a gurgle as Pine grasped at his neck, trying fruitlessly to stem the waterfall of blood pouring from between his claws. He collapsed into the grass, and his foot paws kicked at the dirt.

Humphrey spat out the flesh and brown fur and turned his attention to Benny, a wild look in his eyes and a twisted smile on his blood-soaked lips.

"Gotta go check on the missus, now," Humphrey said and walked away, humming a tune to himself.

Benny was left in silence, staring down at the corpse.

More silence.

Benny found his scream.

Chapter 18

Judgment

"**B**enny, I need you to tell me what happened," York said, holding his son by the shoulders.

Within only a few seconds of hearing Benny's terrified squeak, half of Generocity had surrounded the scene.

"Humphrey . . . it was Humphrey."

"Humphrey? Are you saying Humphrey did this?"

"Where did he go, Benny? Where is he?"

"Humphrey said . . . said he was going to check on his mate."

"His mate? Rose? Oh, no! Pib and Tib, go straight to Rose's burrow, now! Fib, go get Mad."

"The rat? Droppings, York, Pine is— "

"Go get Mad!"

York grabbed a cottonwood leaf and draped it over the corpse. "Don't want any of the young ones to see this."

A few minutes later, Mad came to the scene at a brisk scamper, but upon seeing the pool of blood seeping from underneath the leaf, the rat stopped in his tracks.

"Can you help him, Mad?" York asked.

The rat approached the corpse, raised the leaf, and gave a snort. "Well?"

"What? Oh. That mouse is dead," Mad answered calmly.

"So?" asked York.

"You can't heal dead, Mouse. No one can. Not even the humans." The rat raised the leaf again. "These wounds . . . this was the work of a mouse. Who?"

"My son says it was Humphrey."

"Humphrey? Hmm. That makes sense."

"What do you mean?"

"Rose visited me a few nights back. She is due to have babes."

"So?" Cookie asked. "They had a Mate Vow. They were to have babes sooner or later. Why would he kill . . ." Cookie trailed off. Both his and York's eyes bulged when arriving at the conclusion.

"How did you think Humphrey would react finding Rose had betrayed him?" asked Mad. "Shrug his shoulders and move on? In The Old Code, a mate always stays true."

"That may be what you believe, but for us, the Mate Vow is just a tradition from our ancestors! Not a law! It didn't mean Humphrey had to kill him!" York said.

The rat stroked his whiskers. "True. Well, what are you going to do? What's to happen to Humphrey?"

No mouse spoke, each mind drawing a blank.

The rat sighed, becoming impatient. "May I make a suggestion?"

York looked around at his mouse brethren before conceding with a nod.

"Kill Humphrey."

Cookie, York, Benny, and every other mouse at the scene gasped, horrified by the idea.

"No! Never," replied York. "That would make us no better than the humans. Mice aren't meant to kill each other."

"Someone should have told that to Humphrey," Mad said.

Cookie was about to reply when Pib and Tib appeared, holding Humphrey between them.

"He was headed towards his burrow," informed Tib. "He didn't fight us. I checked on Rose and Crumb and they're okay. I told her to stay in the burrow."

York cautiously approached the blood-stained mouse. "In the name of our Ancestors, why did you do it, Humphrey?"

The mouse did not reply. He only hummed and stared up at the night sky.

"Humphrey? Humphrey? I asked you a question, Humphrey."

Again the mouse did not respond.

"He's mental, that one is," Cookie mumbled. "Maybe that's why he did it? No mouse would kill in his right mind. Mice aren't like that."

Mad burst into laughter.

"This is no laughing matter, Rat," said York.

The rat gained enough control to ask, "So you're not going to kill him?"

York shook his head. "No, we are not like the humans. We are kind creatures. Not murderers. We look after each other."

"Humphrey needs to be made an example of! He made his choice!"

"We do not follow your Old Code, Rat! We do not kill our own!"

"Then what will you do?"

"This poor mouse," York motioned to Humphrey, "does not need punishment. He simply needs," York waved his arms, "he needs love. And rehabilitation."

Again, the rat laughed.

He laughed and laughed and laughed that rock-grinding laugh. He laughed as he left the mice. He laughed as he walked home and laughed as he entered his burrow.

Cookie shook his head. "I don't know who is crazier: Humphrey or that rat?"

The next day, a meeting was held in Generocity to determine the fate of Humphrey. It was quickly agreed that it was a priority to "heal" Humphrey. What would spilling more blood accomplish?

Corn was pulled from the Kindness Pile to pay three mice to carve out a hole in the cottonwood tree where Humphrey would be kept safe while being healed. A stone was rolled to block Humphrey's escape.

It was also agreed more corn would be pulled to enlist an additional defender to guard Humphrey day and night.

When it came time to feed Humphrey, because he could not work, corn was pulled from the Kindness Pile.

If Humphrey became sick, again, corn was pulled from the Kindness Pile to pay the rats for their services.

When a mouse was hired to converse with Humphrey daily to determine whether his mind was healed, corn was pulled from the Kindness Pile.

Such a great society they were, to be so forgiving and so caring for the sick-of-mind.

While Benny and the mice worked in the field, Rose approached York, wiping tears from her eyes with her tail.

"What is it, Rose?" asked York.

"Ever since Humphrey was put into the rehabilitation center, I haven't been earning enough corn as a teacher to take care of myself and Crumb. Worse, I am expecting to give birth next moon. And since . . . and since Pine is dead, and . . . and my mate is stuck in a hole in a tree, they are going to starve!"

"You only teach in the morning," replied Moon, who had been listening in. "Why not harvest in the afternoon and evening in the field? You still have time before the birth to save plenty of corn."

At these words, Rose broke into a fresh wail.

The other mice calmed her, reassuring her it would not come to that.

The rats scoffed. "If she really cared about her family," said Dolley, "she should have thought about the consequences before cheating on her mate and having more babes."

At these words, the mice's patience wore off.

"Leave! Now!" commanded York.

The rats did as they were told. Anyway, they had work to do.

That evening, the mice came together underneath the cottonwood tree and took a vote. Rose, because of her condition, would be able to pull a small amount from the Kindness Pile.

Living in such a generous society filled every mouse in Generocity with pride.

"How kind we are!"

"What a wonderful society we have!"

"Why stop with Rose? Why not allow anyone who is destitute to pull from the Kindness Pile?"

"No mouse would ever have to fear starving again!"

The elders agreed. All that needed to be done was for the mice to contribute more corn every day after harvesting.

Again, a vote was cast, and the motion passed.

"Fools," spat Dolley. "Do you honestly think you can rid a society of fear?"

York gave a firm nod. "Yes, Rat, I believe we can."

The crowd at the base of the cottonwood tree exploded into cheers.

Lint (who had made a full recovery) stepped forward and announced, "I say that we declare today a holiday and celebrate it with song and festivities!"

"What should we call the holiday?" Benny asked from below. He too, was excited by the coming changes.

"Ah, a great question. How about 'No Fear Day,' for we no longer have to fear the hurdles of life!"

The slapping tail applause christened the title, and with a bang of the bottle cap gong, the day was spent in festivities and song.

During the celebration, Benny saw Mad, Dolley, and Moon in the distance, working in the field, harvesting corn.

Chapter 19

No Choice

After the murder of Pine, the mice of Generocity began to notice something strange: even though they worked till midday as usual, after contributing to the pile, only a little less than a quarter of their corn piles remained.

Some, with heavy hearts, returned to the field to work late into the night, fearful of their families starving.

Others approached the elders at midday, declaring hard times had befallen them and they were poor. The elders, of course, allowed them to take what they needed from the Kindness Pile. They thanked the elders and went off and enjoyed the rest of their afternoon with games and songs, their paws laden with corn.

As each day passed, more and more mice would declare poverty and pull from the Kindness Pile. As the poverty rate rose, more and more corn had to be contributed.

Soon, even the elders became confused. Why were so many mice becoming impoverished when there was an entire field of corn just a whisker's breadth away?

Curious indeed.

"What do you mean 'she just showed up?'" whispered York to Rose.

The teacher had difficulty answering him. At the moment, she was struggling to hold onto her babe, Crumb, who fought for freedom, yanking at her fur and screaming at the top of his lungs, desperate to play with his friends.

"Well, it wasn't . . . it wasn't just her," grunted Rose. "It was her mother . . . or at least I think—If you don't stop your struggling, Crumb, you won't get any more playtime!—I think it was her mother. She acted like her mother."

The babe under discussion was playing tag with the other mice of CLAS. She had a white belly and abnormally large eyes and feet. The strange-looking mouse ran and laughed like the rest, unaware of the gaze of the two adults and Benny.

"Did you try asking this 'mother' where they came from? Are they wall-mice? Were they once prisoners of humans, like us?"

For a second, Crumb had escaped Rose's grasp, but a quick lunge on her part prevented his escape. "Gotcha! I tried asking, York. But I couldn't understand a single squeak from that female. And even if I had, she ran away as if I were a cat!"

"Will she come back?"

"I think so. I don't see—*eek!*"

Crumb had climbed onto Rose's shoulders and had taken a firm grasp of her ear . . . with his teeth. She yanked the babe off, throwing him to the ground, and clutched her ear. "That's it! You are no longer playing with the other mice for the rest of today!"

Crumb burst into a fresh scream of fury and bawling.

Rose pointed at the strange-looking babe playing tag and had to shout over Crumb's crying. "What should I do?" Rose asked. "Should I try teaching her like the rest?"

"Of course!" replied York. "We can't just exile babes from Generocity. It's obvious they need our help."

"I suppose. But where did they come from, York?"

York shrugged. "I don't really—"

"I saw a mouse like her," shouted Benny.

The two looked down at him.

"Are you sure, Son?"

Benny nodded. "He had a white belly, just like her. He came from the cornfield."

York frowned. "Well, I guess that explains it: they must be field-mice. I've heard about them before from Lint. Not surprised, really. I'm sure there are more."

"Are we in danger, York?" asked Rose.

"No . . . no, I don't think so. Lint said they're harmless and mind themselves. I think they are just curious of what Generocity offers."

"Oh, they're a danger. You'll see."

All three mice jumped at the voice behind them. It was Dolley, along with six rat babes. Two were jet black, like Mad, and the other four were albino with fierce red eyes like their mother. All six of the babes sat quietly by Dolley, studying the curious scene of Crumb's tantrum.

Benny, used to the rats' company, was the only one not in shock to ask, "How are the field-mice a danger?"

"Did they contribute to the Kindness Pile?"

York gained his senses. "Well, no, I don't think so. But does it matter? It's not the babe's fault her mother didn't donate a few pieces of corn. They probably don't even know about the Kindness Pile."

"It does matter. If they aren't going to contribute, they shouldn't be here."

York sighed, deciding to change the topic. "Dolley, is there anything we can help you with?"

The rat fell silent and cast her gaze down into the dirt, as if . . . ashamed? Yes, Benny thought, it was shame.

"I need to leave my babes here," Dolley mumbled, then quickly added, "but just for today."

Rose's eyes could not widen any further. "All six?"

"Why the change of heart, Dolley?" York asked. "I thought you wanted nothing else but to raise and teach your own babes."

Dolley growled. "If only. But due to the new changes since Pine's murder, my mate is contributing more than ever, and needs my help harvesting." Dolley spat out the word *contribute* as if it were a fresh mouse dropping.

"I don't understand," said York. "Even with the contributions, you still bring in at least two full leaves. Is that not enough?"

"I don't know. Is it enough?"

Rose turned to York with a pleading expression. "I can't take care of them all, York. I mean, six rats?"

"I can assure you it would be easier for a single teacher to care for a whole army of rats like these," Dolley motioned to her six rat babes, "than an army of teachers to care for a mouse like that." Dolley nodded to Crumb, who was throwing dirt at the rat babes.

The rat babes showed little reaction to the dirt clods pelting their faces. Not even a snarl or a hiss.

Dolley had proven her point.

Chapter 20

The Stupidity of The Old Code

Generocity's citizens now numbered in the hundreds due to additional births. Also, more and more of the strange field-mice had appeared from the fields and would drop their babes off at the CLAS and pull food from the Kindness Pile before watching a round of Burrow Rush. The field-mice had happily made themselves at home with the wall-mice and cage-mice.

One fall morning, when Benny stood up to wipe his sweaty brow, he counted only eight other mice that had come to work in the field that morning. (The rats were working as well, but that was to be expected. Rats were greedy.)

There were two mice working close to Benny. There was Twig, who contrary to his name, was quite fat, and Stud, the ex-defender and son of the deceased Pine.

As Twig and Stud worked, Benny could not help but eavesdrop on their conversation.

". . . Trying to earn some extra corn. Ever since I was kicked from the defenders because of my stiff tail, I've been wanting to see what's on the other side of the cornfield, but I need to save food. With my father dead, there's nothing holding me here. I figure if I travel to the other side and back, the defenders will be impressed and let me rejoin their ranks. Why are you out here, Twig?"

"My mate, Pearl, is making me," said Twig, huffing deeply from his snout, his weight making it difficult to breathe. "She says there is no pride in pulling from the Kindness Pile like the others. She says it's 'a bad example for the babes.'" Twig grabbed a harvested corn kernel and stuffed it into one of his cheeks, talking as he chewed. "I say, why 'ot 'ull from the 'indness 'ile? Everyone else is? Why break my back? Isn't 'at why"—Twig swallowed—"it's there? I swear, if I could just leave her and those brats, I would be the happiest mouse alive."

"Why don't you?"

Benny's ears perked up, intrigued by Stud's suggestion.

Twig paused in his work and slowly chewed the corn in his mouth, considering the option. "Really? Just leave her? I . . . I couldn't. What would the other mice think?"

"Rose cheated on Humphrey by sleeping with my father, and no one seemed to care . . . well, except for Humphrey, the piece of filth."

"The rats cared," replied Twig. "They said she didn't deserve to pull from the Kindness Pile after Humphrey was placed into rehabilitation. Said she broke The Old Code and should have stayed true to—"

"Are you kiddin'?" interrupted Stud. "No one listens to those creatures. They're all about following that Old Code. It's just a bunch of pointless rules. In fact, in order to follow this Old Code, I hear the rats still bite their babes' tails for punishment."

"No!" Corn sprayed from Twig's engorged mouth. "Last time I heard of the practice of tail-biting was when Grand Pappy did it to my father! And back in Grand Pappy's time, mice acted like such . . . such . . ."

"Savages?" suggested Stud.

"Yeah. Savages. Are you sure that the rats still do that?"

"It's true. Rose told me." Stud gave a confident nod. "No, Twig, don't worry what the rats think. You should do what makes you happy; isn't that what it means to be free: to do what makes you happy?"

Twig, the fat mouse, took another bite of corn and chewed, pondering Stud's words. "You know, that's not the only thing I've been thinking of. What if, instead of working in the field, I do what Benny is doing and—"

"Shhh. He's right over there," Stud whispered.

However, Benny continued shucking an ear of corn, pretending he had not heard his name.

Twig lowered his voice. "I heard Benny is having the rats teach him how to heal. I thought about doing the same thing. Have you seen how much mice are paying the rats!"

"You're telling me," said Stud, glancing back at his tail. "That rat spent just a few minutes strapping my tail to a stick and charged me a whole four leaves."

"See? That's what I mean," exclaimed Twig. "After learning from the rats, I wouldn't have to sweat my tail off in this stinkin' field ever again."

"Why don't you go ask them right now?" Stud nodded towards the direction of the rats. "I bet the rats wouldn't mind teaching you."

"Well . . ."

"Come on, don't be scared of 'em."

"Well, alright."

Benny watched Twig hobble his way to the rats.

The rats paused what they were doing and slowly turned and faced the fat mouse. For a few minutes, Twig did all the talking, and the rats only stared at him. Mad said something and went back to work.

Twig walked back, his whiskers drooping and tail dragging in the dirt.

"Well, what did they say?" asked Stud. "What did they say?"

Twig shook his head. "Oh . . . oh nothing," he muttered.

However, Benny knew what Mad had requested.

As the day wore on, Stud had finished gathering his two leaves.

"Well, that's it for me. Should be enough. You coming, Twig?"

"No . . . no, I think I will stay out here a bit longer."

"Really? You have plenty. Come on."

"No, I think I'll keep working."

"Fine by me. See you tomorrow."

As Benny worked, Twig began to talk to himself, whispering over and over, "A whole leaf of corn? A whole leaf of corn? Those greedy sacks of droppings. A whole blasted leaf of corn . . ."

It was not until the last ray of sunlight disappeared that Twig bit himself on the tongue while gnawing at the base of a stalk and cursed, "Blast this corn, and blast those blasted rats! I'm done. This is insane! Why would anyone want to work this hard just for some extra corn!"

Twig furiously piled up what little corn he had harvested and began making his exit. When passing Benny, Twig paused long enough to mutter to the small black mouse, "Those rats are going to work you to death, Benny."

Benny ignored Twig's words and continued harvesting. He dreamed of piles of corn.

The next morning, Cookie rushed into York and Benny's burrow. "York, we found something. Come see."

York, accompanied by Benny and Hazel, followed close to Cookie as they headed into the cornfield, the morning mist making visibility limited.

As they scampered across the ground, Cookie explained, "Last night, Pib heard a group of humans in the field. Either Pib was really stupid—or really brave—but he went and investigated."

"Are the humans still there?"

"No, they left a little while ago. Pib and Lint are there now. They believe the humans were just passing through."

"The humans are gone? So what's the problem?"

"Well, York, they left something behind."

At that moment, they entered a clearing of crushed cornstalks. In the middle was a smoldering fire, filled with charred beer cans (similar to what had been used for the Kindness Pile), glass bottles, and cigarette butts.

Pib and Lint were standing next to this heap of half-burnt trash, studying one particular bottle. As the four approached, Lint was jabbing at the bottle with his cane, watching as a clear, amber liquid swished back and forth inside the unopen vessel.

"What is it?" York asked.

"Whiskey."

The answer came from behind, causing the mice to jump. It was Mad.

"For the love of the Ancestors, can't you rats approach from the front for once!" York shouted, a paw over his heart.

"How did you know about this?" Lint asked, glaring at the rat.

"I was harvesting corn and saw those four scuttling by," said the rat. "Don't often see mice come into the field this early to work anymore. I figured it was important."

Benny's attention was still drawn to the large bottle. "What did you say it was called, Mad?"

"Whiskey."

"Is it dangerous?" Cookie asked, backing away from the bottle.

"It didn't seem dangerous to the humans," said Pib. "I watched them all night, and they loved the stuff."

Mad snorted. "They won't be loving it when they wake up."

"What makes you say that, Mad," asked York.

"Younger Brother Human snuck one of these bottles into his room. He drank only a little, but the next morning, he looked like he wanted to die."

"Why would humans drink such a thing?" asked Cookie, staring in disgust at the bottle.

"Because he's a liar," said Lint. "I know what you're up to, Rat. You just want it all for yourself. This," Lint extended his paws to the bottle as if desiring to embrace a long lost brother, "is nothing like what the rat describes."

"You've seen this before?" asked York.

"Seen it? I've had it!"

The surrounding rodents gasped.

"When I was young, I was going through the human's trash. I found a container, just like this, with a few drops left."

"And you were a fool enough to try it?" asked Mad.

"Yes, Rat, I did. Unlike you, I'm not a coward when it comes to trying new things. And let me tell you, that liquid made me feel stronger than a thousand mice and smarter than a human . . . if only I could describe it to you!" Even at that moment, Lint began smacking his lips, as if overcome by a great thirst.

Benny approached the bottle and saw his distorted reflection. It scared him.

The black rat stepped forward. "York, for the sake of Generocity, you must pour it out. No good will come from this. The Old Code warns of it."

"Pour it out?" screeched Lint. "You can take that Old Code and shove it right up your tail!" The old mouse waved his cane and charged at the rat, but Pib stepped in between them. Lint turned to York. "Are we not free? What is freedom without pleasure! Don't you want to be happy? If only I could describe what it is like! Just try some, York. Just a little, and you'll see who is right."

"What do you want to do, York?" asked Cookie. "Should we bring it back to Generocity, or do what the rat says and dispose of the stuff?"

York looked at Hazel. His daughter was curiously sniffing the bottle.

He made his decision.

Later that afternoon, out in the cornfield, Benny was halfway to harvesting another full leaf when a chaos of loud squeaks came from the direction of Generocity. He stopped what he was doing and began rushing towards the city, fearing for his sister and father.

Moon suddenly blocked his path. "Where do you think you're going? You have work to do if you want to learn from my father."

"Don't you hear the screams? They're in trouble! It's probably a opossum that's—"

"Those aren't screams, Mouse."

Benny listened more closely. The rat was right: it was laughter. Pure, riotous, hysterical laughter.

"Is . . . is it because of the whiskey?"

Moon said nothing, going back to work on her corncob.

"It *is* the whiskey. I . . . I think I'll go and take a quick peek to see what is going on. Just to make sure they're fine."

"They sound just dandy to me," Moon, said, pulling at the corn. "Stay. You have work to do."

"But I even saw field-mice going to Generocity to try the whiskey. Everyone is there. Can't we work some other day?"

"Go back to work, Benny," the rat repeated.

"Why should I listen to you? I'm free to do what I want, aren't I?"

"The Old Code condemns such—"

That did it for Benny. "No one wants to follow your stupid Old Code!"

Moon paused. She twitched her whiskers and swished her tail.

Benny was expecting the white rat to attack, or at the very least yell at him.

Instead, Moon quietly said, "You're right, Benny. You're right." It was the first time Moon had said his name. "You don't have to follow The Old Code. If you don't believe in it, what's stopping you? Go on. Go and enjoy your freedom like the rest . . . if that's what you think freedom is. If that's what you think happiness is. If you think whiskey and feasting will bring you peace, go on. Go and seek it."

Moon went back to work.

"I'm not like you! I'm not a rat! I'm . . . I'm a mouse!"

"I know you are, Benny."

"I'll never be like you! I'll never be a rat!" And with that, he scampered off to join his mouse brethren.

The bottle of whiskey had been dragged into the center of Generocity. There it stood, like a god, overlooking all of the festivities.

The drink burned Benny's throat like fire. After a few minutes, the guilt of leaving Moon alone in the cornfield no longer plagued his conscience. In fact, he felt wonderful!

A white-bellied field-mouse, whom Benny had never met, appeared from within the crowd. The mouse gave Benny a flirtatious lick on the cheek and then poured more of the whiskey down his throat from a seed shell as onlookers cheered on.

Chapter 21

Blood Suckers

"**C**ome, Son, it's time to wake up."

Benny's bloodshot eyes fluttered open.

It was his father. "The person who is in charge of picking up the babes for CLAS is passed out, so I dropped your sister off at—what in the Ancestors! You smell like dung, Benny!" Benny looked down to discover he was lying in a puddle of vomit . . . or was it urine?

He took a whiff and turned his head, coughing at the smell. It was both.

York pinched his own snout as he talked. "Anyways, I have to go to the rats' burrow. Some mice are injured, and the rats are being . . . disagreeable. Since you are friends with the rats, you could—"

"I'm not friends with 'em." Benny muttered as he struggled to find his legs.

"Well, either way, you're coming."

"Can . . . can I go wash in the stream first?"

"No, it can't wait."

The two walked to the rats' burrow where a crowd of mice awaited medical attention. Some groaned. Others licked their wounds from fights they did not remember. Occasionally, a mouse would fall to his knees and puke. Benny realized, even with his vomit-and-urine-encrusted fur, amongst these pitiful creatures, he was right at home.

At the front of the line stood Mad. He was silent as several mice yelled at him.

"What seems to be the matter here?" York approached the front.

One of the mice, whose left side of his face was completely swollen, pointed an accusing finger at the rat. "He's charging a half a leaf just to look at my eye!"

"And a full leaf of corn to fix my ear," piped up another mouse, holding dirt to an ear, partially bitten off in a fight.

York grimaced at the sight of both mice's wounds. "Well, pay him then."

Swollen-eye looked down, ashamed. "I . . . I can't."

"Why not? I've heard both of you brag about how much you have saved up."

The two mice glanced at each other. "Well, umm . . . last night . . . we don't know what we were thinking, but, well, we . . ."

Torn-ear interceded for his friend. "Well, you see, it was just so crazy last night. We got ahead of ourselves, and—"

"They spent it all on the booze," said Mad, crossing his paws in front of his chest.

"All of it?" asked York.

Swollen-Eye and Torn-Ear nodded.

"The same goes for the rest of them," muttered the rat.

York glanced around. "Is this true?"

They all nodded.

York sighed. "Well, I'll tell Cookie to bring corn from the Kindness Pile. It's not right that you all suffer. I just hope you learned your lesson."

"Oh, York, trust us. We have."

Mad sighed. "This isn't right."

"Mad, you know that's why the Kindness Pile exists," said York. "And why are you complaining? You're the one profiting."

"With what I'll have to contribute to make up for their folly, no, I won't be."

"Please, Mad, I am in no mood to argue. Just do as you're told. I'm sure this event will never be repeated. Do you honestly think these mice will willingly get drunk as before? What fools do you take them for?"

"It was against The Old Code."

A few mice groaned at the comment, and others rolled their eyes.

"I understand you don't agree, but doesn't your Old Code at least mention forgiveness?"

Mad took a deep breath. "Fine, but I'll need your son's help."

Benny looked up. "What?"

York gave a sigh of relief and pushed his son forward. "Perfect. Well, I'll be back. I have some business to attend to. Thanks for helping, Benny." And with that, York headed off.

Mad shoved rags and bandages into Benny's chest. "I'll take care of the bad ones. You get the others. Time to make some corn." Mad was about to turn away but grabbed Benny's paw and gave it a whiff. The rat scowled. "Clean your paws first or you'll kill 'em with infection."

Benny did as he was told.

Most of the wounds required a small bandage or a few stitches. Benny was surprised at how resourceful he was, as were the other mice.

"Benny, I think I'll come to see you from now on," said Stud as Benny cleaned a scratch on his arm.

The last patient was a field-mouse who revealed a nasty wound on his white belly.

Mad turned from the field-mouse and began packing up his things. The field-mouse, baffled at why he was not being healed like the others, began to chatter angrily in his confusing language. The rat ignored him and continued cleaning up his supplies.

The frantic squeaking grabbed the attention of York, who had just returned.

"Mad? You're not finished. This mouse needs your assistance!"

"I'm not helping him," said the rat, not looking up from his supplies. "At least the other mice contributed something. The field-mice don't. They just come here to take from the Kindness Pile."

"It doesn't matter," said York. "Take care of him.

"No."

"I find your intolerance for field-mice sickening, Mad."

"I don't have an intolerance for white-bellies."

"Ah, ah, ah!" York interjected with a raised paw. "Please. Call them field-mice. We feel the name 'white-bellies' is so derogatory."

"Fine. I don't have an intolerance for whi—I mean field-mice. I have an intolerance for leeches."

"A leech? Is that how you see the sick and needy?"

"No, just the needy who don't work for what they need."

"Please, Mad, we are paying you several leaves of corn."

"It's not *your* corn. It belongs to those who worked for it. And it wouldn't be an issue if you hadn't been a bunch of drunken fools the night before. The Old Code is clear what happens to drunkards in the afterlife."

"Enough, Mad."

"It's a place of misery and pain and—"

"Enough!" York shouted. "If you do not do what I ask and follow the laws . . ." He motioned with his paw and two defenders stepped forward.

Mad took the hint and healed the field-mouse.

Chapter 22

Think of the Babes

Mad charged York seven leaves of corn for healing the mice that morning.

York brought Mad the payment. "I already took the liberty of contributing a portion of your payment to the Kindness Pile." With that, York handed over only a half a leaf of corn.

Mad stared at it for a second, then without saying a word, split half of the pathetic payment with Benny and left.

It was Benny's first payment for healing. For doctoring over a dozen mice, he had expected more than just a quarter of a leaf. It was barely enough to buy whiskey; the defenders guarding the bottle charged five kernels for a single shell filled with the fiery liquid.

"Father, where does the corn go that is spent on whiskey?"

"It will go to funding the CLAS and helping Rose."

"Shouldn't that have been put to a vote for Generocity to decide?" asked Benny.

York cocked an eyebrow and stroked a whisker. "Do you think any mouse would be opposed to such an idea?"

York was right. No mouse would be opposed to the idea.

"Ah, speaking of Rose," said York, changing the topic, "She gave birth this morning. I thought it would be nice of us to bring her a leaf of corn from the Kindness Pile."

Benny looked back at the quarter leaf of corn and thought back to his dreams of earning mountains of food through healing.

"Benny, did you hear me? Let's go bring Rose her full leaf of corn from the Kindness Pile."

Rose was on her side, nursing the three babes when York and Benny stepped in. She put on a weak smile, an ineffective attempt to hide her weariness. "It's so good to see you." Her voice was as weak as her smile. "Is that for me?" She nodded to the leaf full of corn Benny dragged in.

"From the Kindness Pile," said York.

"Oh, just wonderful. Please, put it right over there with the others."

"How has it been, Rose?" York asked.

"Oh, it's . . . it's been rough. It's not like when I had Crumb. At least Humphrey was there to help me. I hear he might be released from rehabilitation?"

York nodded. "Yes. I met with his mind healer yesterday. She says when Humphrey heard of your upcoming birth, he broke down into tears. Apparently, Humphrey wants to apologize. It sounds promising. Lint, Cookie, and I are going to talk to him later this afternoon. If his mind is truly healed, he will be freed from the confines of the cottonwood tree. Would you like to be there when we make the decision?"

Rose shook her head. "No. No, I'll be fine. I have to stay here with the babes. Could you tell him I'm waiting here and that . . . that I'm ready to forgive him?"

"I would be happy to," said York with a comforting smile.

"Maybe things can finally go back to normal."

York sat down next to her. "Speaking of 'going back,' when will you be able to teach again?"

"Why, is something wrong?"

"No. Everything is fine. Pebble is watching the CLAS. She's a natural teacher," reassured York. "However, Pebble said this morning the babes were a little rowdy. She's having a meeting with Dolley over an incident involving Crumb and one of the rat babes."

"Oh, no. Did a rat hurt my baby?"

York eased her down. "Pebble didn't say, but I'm sure she will handle it appropriately."

Rose placed a paw onto York's. "Could you please go to the cinderblock and make sure Crumb is okay?"

"I don't know if I will have enough time, Rose." He caught her pitiful stare. "But if I have time after Humphrey's verdict, I'll stop by and listen in."

"Thank you, York," Rose said, patting his paw. "Actually, I wanted to talk to you about Crumb. My babe is falling behind in learning how to count and won't listen to a word I say about our history. In fact, I have noticed it from a majority of the babes. Obviously, we don't want them to fall behind in their studies. So, I thought when I am better, Pebble can stay and help teach."

"Another teacher?"

"Well, no. Just someone to be there to help Crumb and any other babe struggling. I don't think it's the babes' fault. I think, deep down, every mouse wants to learn. I think they just need extra guidance."

York gave her a comforting smile. "I think no babe ever having to fear failure is a great idea."

York stood up and turned to leave.

"Oh, and York, one other thing."

York sighed. "Yes?"

"The babes are supposed to bring their own lunch to CLAS, but for the last couple of weeks, the babes are bringing barely anything. I thought the CLAS could start providing free meals to all the babes whose families can't afford it. I hate seeing the babes starve. It's not their fault they've fallen on rough times."

York nodded. "I agree. I'll bring it up in the next Generocity meeting. I'm sure all the mice will agree to donate more corn to the Kindness Pile."

"Oh, bless you, York." Rose closed her eyes and laid her head down into the grass bedding, a weak smile on her face. "You've been the closest thing to a brother. I don't know who else to go to. Please, don't forget to go to my son's meeting."

"I won't."

"And don't forget to tell Humphrey what I said."

"Get some sleep, Rose."

She let out a long breath, her eyes fluttering shut. "Everything will finally go back to normal."

Chapter 23

Success

$\mathbf{F}$or the rest of the afternoon, Benny worked in the field. Including himself, there were five mice harvesting.

Benny supposed the other mice of Generocity had stayed home to rest their wounds and headaches from the night before. Or they were sick. Yes, it was getting colder. That must be it. They were getting cold and becoming sick.

Suddenly, the fat mouse Twig came huffing by, shouting, "They're making their decision about Humphrey! They're making their decision about Humphrey!"

Curious, Benny headed towards the cottonwood tree. There, the meeting was already in session. A large group of mice surrounded the elders and Humphrey. The murderous mouse stood between two defenders.

He heard his father announce the elders' decision:

". . . And since the mind healer has seen great change in your behavior, and because of your expression of sorrow, the elders and I are happy to receive you back into Generocity!"

Lint gave the bottle cap a bang, signaling the conclusion of the verdict, and there was a cheer.

Humphrey beamed with excitement and tears ran down his face as the two defenders patted him on the back in congratulations.

Was this well-groomed, happy mouse really the cold-blooded murderer that Benny had seen tear open Pine's throat?

It was true! The rehabilitation system was a success!

Chapter 24

Abuse

Y ork asked Benny to follow him to the meeting at the cinderblock. "I need you to pick up your sister."

"I thought someone else was supposed to take Hazel home?"

"He's still at his burrow, sick from last night's festivities."

Benny groaned, but a stern look from his father silenced him.

When Benny and York arrived at the cinderblock, despite how late it was, countless babes ran about. Dolley, Pebble, Crumb, and a white rat babe stood next to the block. The two adults were talking. Hazel stood a little ways off, giggling with friends as they pounced onto freshly fallen leaves, crunching them into bits.

Crumb was crying.

The white rat babe stood silently by his mother's side, glaring at the blubbering mouse.

"Fighting is a huge no-no, Dolley," said Pebble. "And John, your son, will not even apologize to Crumb."

"Crumb said we didn't deserve our corn!" the white rat babe shouted.

Dolley hissed at John. "What have I told you about interrupting adults!"

The white rat babe cast his gaze at the ground, "Sorry, Pebble."

Pebble caught sight of York and Benny. "Oh, I'm sorry, York. I'm just a little busy at the moment."

"Actually, that's why we're here. Rose requested I listen in on her behalf. Would that be alright?"

"I think that's perfectly fine. Dolley, are you okay with this?"

The rat had an annoyed frown. "If that is what Rose wants."

"So what happened?" York asked.

"Well, after lunch, I was busy with another babe when I heard Crumb squealing for help. I found John on top of Crumb, practically trying to claw his eyes out."

"I was just asking John if he thought Mad would . . . would help our family since . . . since we are so po . . . pooooor!" Crumb sobbed.

"You dumb liar! That's not what you—"

Before the rat babe could finish his statement, Dolley had leaned behind and given her son a nip on the tail, causing the rat babe to yipe in pain.

Pebble and York were horrified.

"Dolley, what are you doing to your son?" York asked.

"I'm disciplining him. He knows better than to speak to others like that."

"But biting your son on the tail?" asked Pebble. "Don't you think that is a bit much?"

"It's how my mother raised me, and my mother's mother raised her. It's what The Old Code tells—"

"Yes, yes," interrupted York. "We know. But there are more . . . civilized ways to punish babes."

"Really? Like what?"

"Well, there are timeouts, and . . . and . . ."

"My mother doesn't bite my tail," announced Crumb, jabbing a thumb at his chest. "When I'm good, she gives me a treat, like extra corn."

York ruffled the fur on Crumb's head. "There you go: extra corn. An incentive to be good."

Dolley took a step back, looking at them like they were lunatics. "Reward them? For doing what is expected?"

"Maybe, Dolley," Pebble suggested as delicately as possible, "your babe is starting fights because of the abuse he receives at home?"

"But I didn't start the—" Again, John was silenced by another quick nip on the tail by his mother.

"For our Ancestors' sake, Rat! Will you stop that cruel behavior!" Pebble shrieked. "I won't have it! Not in my CLAS. Have you no heart? York, do something about this!"

"I agree with Pebble, Dolley," York said, stepping forward. "It's not what a loving parent does."

"It's exactly what a loving parent does, and again, these are my babes, and I will raise them any way I see fit. It is commanded by The Old Code. Am I not free?"

"Not if your Old Code commands you to abuse your babes," York said firmly.

"Are you serious?" Dolley looked at both of them, almost amused. "And what are you going to do? Take them away from me?"

York was stone-faced.

"Oh, dear Ancients . . ." Dolley's one eye widened.

York shook his head and laughed. "Listen, I'm sure it will never come to that. Let's just have these young ones apologize to each other and move on with our day, hmm?"

Crumb rubbed a foot-paw in the dirt as he wringed his pink tail between his paws. "I'm . . . I'm sorry that . . . that I asked for help from your really rich family. I know you need the corn more than the rest . . ." But poor Crumb could not finish his sentence due to the fresh onslaught of tears of shame.

John stepped forward, opened his mouth, but then shut it and glanced back at the hard gaze of his mother. John sighed and cast a defeated stare at the ground. "I'm sorry I fought you."

York patted both babes' shoulders. "There, now. That wasn't so hard, was it?"

Pebble approached Dolley with an outstretched paw. "Thank you so much for coming, Dolley. I know how busy you and your mate are."

Dolley looked at the paw and hesitantly reached out her own.

As they shook, Dolley's rough, calloused claws hid the delicate pink flesh of Pebble's paw. "It was a pleasure, Pebble. I am never too busy for my babes. They come first in my life."

"I'm sure," said Pebble with a forced smile.

With that, Dolley turned, taking John with her.

Only Benny saw Crumb stick his tongue out and make faces at the rats as they left.

York released a breath. "I'm not jealous of your job, Pebble, especially when dealing with their type."

"Actually, I am quite surprised," replied the substitute teacher. "Rose informed me the rat babes were generally well-behaved. Really, they are my best students. However, after today, and seeing how their parents abuse them . . . I have to say, York, I'm worried about their safety."

York nodded to Crumb. The babe quickly ceased making faces and pretended to wipe tears from his eyes. "How about we get this young one home first?"

"Oh, I don't need help. I can walk home on my own," said Crumb proudly.

Before York could reply, Crumb had already scampered down the hill.

York turned to Rose, chuckling, "What a splendid babe. In fact, I think Crumb had a good point about the rats."

"What do you mean?" asked Pebble.

"About how rich they are. Yet they don't give any corn to those in need?"

"Oh, York, those rats would never give it up."

"They have this silly idea of believing something is theirs, just because they earned it. How would our society survive if we followed that logic? Who would take care of the sick and the old? How would we educate our young? How would we defend ourselves?"

"And those dreadful tail-bitings!" exclaimed, Pebble.

"Indeed. I'll be talking to the elders about it tonight. I'm sure—"

A scream broke across the silent afternoon of Generocity.

Hazel grabbed Benny's paw, frightened.

"What was that?" gasped Pebble.

"It sounded like Crumb," said York.

A moment later, Pib and Tib ran up to Pebble and York.

"Where is the rat, Dolley?" asked Pib, panting.

Benny felt Hazel yank a tuft of his fur. She was pointing at the two defenders' paws.

They were red. Blood.

"We...we just spoke with her," stammered York. "I think she headed back to the field to work. Why? What did the rats do? What's—"

"Mad needs Dolley's help at Rose's burrow," said Pib. He pointed to Benny. "He also asked for your son."

"Is something wrong?" asked Pebble.

"It's Humphrey...he...," Pib tried to keep his composure, but it was too much, and the words burst from his mouth in a terrible moan: "Ancestors above! Humphrey's killed them all! He's killed them all!"

Chapter 25

Picking Up the Pieces

Mad didn't need Benny's help saving lives. Mad needed help cleaning up the mess.

Humphrey was dragged back to the rehabilitation room in the cottonwood tree, laughing hysterically.

Benny spent the rest of the night by the stream, desperately scrubbing with a leaf to wash the blood off his fur and paws.

Chapter 26

The Final Solution

The next evening, the three remaining elder mice, Cookie, Lint, and York, called for a meeting.

As the crowd gathered below, the three stood on the lowest branch of the cottonwood tree, looking down upon the citizens of Generocity.

A large group of field-mice was sectioned in the back. The field-mice babes who attended CLAS had learned the language of the Generocitians, and for the past week had acted as their parents' translators.

Next to the field-mice, the rats were perched on the tree root jutting up from the ground. Moon was scowling. Dolley drew her rat babes close, her tail twitching nervously. And Mad? Mad had no expression at all.

There was an air of excitement. Every rodent could sense it. Tonight would be a time of change.

York moved forward to the very tip of the branch. There was no need for Lint to bang the gong. The crowd immediately fell silent.

"My fellow citizens of Generocity, we were prisoners, and not just those kept in cages by the humans. I mean all of us: field-mice, cage-mice, wall-mice, and rats. What were we prisoners of? Fear! Fear of starvation. Fear of opossums. Fear of being old and helpless. Fear of not having shelter. But now, because of the Kindness Pile, generosity and equality have eliminated these fears—"

The crowd burst into a cheer that made Benny's ears ring. He squeaked along with them.

With a motion of his paws, York calmed them. "Yes, but you did not let me finish. We have eliminated these fears . . . but not all."

The crowd murmured.

"What else is there to be afraid of?" came a random shout.

Benny's father raised a single digit on his paw. "First is the fear for your babes' future. No longer. The CLAS and its teachers will take care of them. They will feed them, teach them, and shelter them. Someone will stop by your burrow, drop them off at the cinderblock, and they will be looked after the entire day. No longer do you have to fear for your babe's wellbeing except for at night. Of course, this will all be funded by the Kindness Pile.

"Second," he emphasized, raising a second claw, "there is the fear of violence. Sometimes, mice cannot control the way they think and will do . . . horrible things. Why did Rose and her family die? Was it because of Humphrey? Of course not. He cannot be blamed. It is because he had these!" York extended his paw. "Claws! Sharp, dangerous claws! If Humphrey did not have claws, Rose and her family's death could have been prevented. So, starting tonight, all mice who live in Generocity will dull their claws by rubbing them against stone. Cookie, himself, has already tested the method. Show them."

Cookie stepped forward and revealed to the crowd his claws, which indeed had been filed to dull nubs.

"Does it hurt?" someone asked.

"Not at all," Cookie shouted down.

"But how will we protect ourselves from the opossum?"

"That's what the defenders are for. Only the defenders, and the defenders alone will be allowed to keep their claws," replied York.

What an ingenious idea! thought the mice. No claws, no killing. So simple.

"We will keep our claws!" shouted Moon.

York laughed. "Did you not hear what I said? Defenders will protect all of Generocity from harm."

"But who will protect us from the defenders?" Moon asked. "Who will protect us from Generocity?"

With a wave, York dismissed Moon's nonsensical statement and continued. "However, claws are not Generocity's biggest threat, which brings me to my next point: greed. We must destroy greed. For there are those in our midst who take advantage of the weak in order to prosper."

A few heads turned in the rats' direction.

"Just a little while ago, I sent defenders to search the rats' burrow."

"You had no right!" Moon shouted up at the elders, a fire in her pink eyes.

Mad said nothing. Instead, he only tilted his head slightly to the side, as if intrigued by what the mice had done.

"Right?" York laughed. "What about the rights of the mice who are starving because you keep all the corn to yourself?" York called down to the base of the tree. "Bring out the rats' corn!"

From behind the tree trunk, multiple defenders appeared, dragging hundreds of leaves of corn. Enough corn to fill the Kindness Pile twenty times over!

The crowd burst into whispers. Whispers transformed into booing, and soon, the whole crowd turned their attention to the rats, yelling and shouting curses. Dolley herded her rat babes behind her and Moon hissed, her white fur bristling.

But still, Mad remained silent.

"Peace! Peace!" shouted York.

The crowd obeyed.

"Yes, greed is a poison. A poison that steals from the many to satisfy the few. We wondered where all the corn had gone. Well, there you have it," he said, pointing to the leaves of corn piled between the crowd and the base of the cottonwood tree. "For this great society to progress, it is crucial all is shared. From now on, whatever is gathered from the cornfield will be contributed to the Kindness Pile. All of it. In return, every day, every citizen of Generocity will receive ten corn kernels."

"We'll receive ten kernels, no matter what?" someone asked.

"No matter what," responded York. "Already you are contributing more than half your leaves. By contributing the rest, we can all rest assured that no one can be taken advantage of. No longer will there be wealthy, and no longer will there be poor. Only the middle class. Greed will finally be defeated."

Dolley's mouth gaped open at the news, and she blinked her one eye in disbelief. "You're insane!"

"I'm insane? This, coming from the mother who abuses her babes?"

"Tail-biting is not abuse. It's how we teach them right from wrong. It is demanded by The Old Code."

"Ah," York rubbed his paws together. "Which brings me to the last fear: The Old Code." He said the words *Old Code* like one talks about rot and filth. "Many complaints have been brought to the elders that you have condemned actions of mice, saying that when they die, they will be tormented in an afterlife. Is this true?"

Mad bowed his head in a nod. "Yes. It is true."

Members in the crowd shook their heads in disgust.

"Such a horrid notion! Just because mice wish to do what makes them happy?" York said. "Here we are, trying to do our best to get rid of fear, while you and your Old Code incite it!"

"Are you saying we are no longer free to follow The Old Code," asked Dolley, "the whole purpose for which we escaped the humans and came here?"

"No, no, no," York replied, holding up his paws in defense. "You may follow The Old Code, but from now on, you can no longer speak of The Old Code in public or commit actions of The Old Code which another member of Generocity would find offensive."

Moon gave a snarl and leapt off the root. "All we wanted was freedom!"

The defenders had waited for this moment. They made their way through the crowd, pushing mice aside.

Faster than the twitch of a whisker, Mad stood in his daughter's path.

Moon bent her head. "Father, I'm sorry. I'm just . . . I'm just sick of—"

Mad leaned forward and whispered something into his daughter's ear.

Moon stared at her father for a second and walked back to her mother and siblings on the root.

As the defenders muscled their way through the crowd, Mad casually faced them. He lifted a paw, halting Tib and Fib. "Thank you, but your assistance is no longer required." Mad looked up towards the branch. "York, will you please accept my apologies for my daughter's rude behavior?"

"Of course," York said, regaining his composure. "As long as there are no other outbursts."

"There will be no other outburst. However, although the solutions you have provided are . . . interesting, may I please have the chance to suggest a different path?"

There was a pause, and all heads swiveled up to the elders to see their decision.

Lint smacked his gums and growled. His opinion was obvious.

Cookie whispered something to York. York nodded, and flashed a smile down to the rat. "Yes, Mad, you are free to come up to the branch and speak."

Mad walked through the hateful stares and muttered curses, and climbed up the trunk and across the branch.

"Be quick about it, Rat," muttered Lint.

As Mad opened his mouth, there began a chorus of booing and jeers.

York stepped forward, laughing. "Now, now, let him speak! Let him speak!"

A few members in the crowd snorted. How silly this was, listening to a rat, but they did as they were told.

Mad gave York a courteous nod of thanks. He turned his gaze back to the mice and, in that rough, stone-grinding voice, spoke to the mice of Generocity.

Chapter 27

Mad's Speech

"**Y**ou wish to get rid of fear, an idea that is understandable and one I wish I could support, however, I cannot. You see, fear and desire are gifts. They are the great motivators. Motivators that if destroyed will halt the progress of society. If you wish to be free, there must exist the fear of failure and the desire of success. Instead of the steps taken by York and the elders, I suggest a different path: eliminate the Kindness Pile."

At this, there was a large gasp from the crowd.

Mad continued. "Let us not be a city of forced sharing and absolute equality, for these two ideas are seeds to producing the sloth and the fool. Instead, let us be a city of self-reliance and plant the seed of independence and liberty.

"But now, I must speak of The Old Code. Not once did I say that you had to follow its ways. Never. The Old Code specifically mentions you can follow it, or not. You see, even the Ancients recognized freedom of choice as a gift.

"Yes, I did condemn certain actions, but if you do not believe in The Old Code, then why should you listen to what I say? If there is no life after death, what do you have to fear if I am wrong? Simply push me to the side and ignore my words.

"But, mice, I must warn you, The Old Code is the only unwavering standard of morality. Without The Old Code, it will be impossible to live in a free democratic society, for our nature and beliefs shape a democracy's laws. And, unfortunately, at our true nature, we are violent and desire immediate pleasure. This is proven, for even at a young age we must be taught restraint and self-control. If we are to rely on our own twisted nature and foolish wisdom to create laws, we will construct a world of chaos.

"I ask—no I beg of you—follow The Old Code. Eliminate the Kindness Pile. Have choice. Have freedom. With fear and desire, every mouse will push to learn, invent, work, and produce. We will not just survive. We will thrive."

Chapter 28

Murderers

With this, Mad ended his speech and fell back behind the elders, leaving the crowd below in an eerie silence. Benny heard the rustling of the cottonwood's leaves. An owl hooted. A single cricket chirped in the distance.

"What a load of dung!"

The comment came from somewhere within the crowd, but it did not matter from whom. It was merely the spark. The mice around Benny erupted into shouts of rage. They cursed, they booed, they screamed. They whipped their tails, stirring the dust. They hated, and they despised. They tore at their fur and spittle sprayed from their mouths.

"Greedy rats!"

"Get rid of the Kindness Pile! Are they insane?"

"Selfish rats!"

"Opinionated rats!"

"Brainwashing rats!"

"Cruel rats!"

"Unloving rats!"

"Punish them!"

"Kill them!"

"Judging rats!"

"Kill them!"

"Kill them!"

"Kill them!"

It became a chant. Even the babes joined in, skipping in circles as they sang the words. "Kill the rats. Kill the rats. Kill the rats . . ."

Only the three elders and Benny stayed silent. Benny was scared. The elders, evident by their smiles, were satisfied by the crowd's rejection of Mad's speech.

Lint banged the gong several times until the crowd quieted. The mice around Benny wiped the foam from their lips, panting.

"Well, then," said York, stepping forward, rubbing his paws together. "There you have it. Do as the elders have suggested and simply contribute all to the Kindness Pile, leave your babes at CLAS, dull your claws, and live a life free from poverty, violence, and fear . . . or eliminate the Kindness Pile so that the poor, weak, and helpless starve."

Lint took York's place on the branch to tally the vote. "If you desire to follow the elders' path, raise your—"

Before Lint finished, every mouse paw, including Benny's, shot up, and there was an ear-ringing cheer. They patted themselves on the back, shook paws, and laughed with joy. It was indeed a momentous day.

More bangs of the bottle cap gong forced the mass silent. "Hold your whiskers!" commanded Lint, but even he had a smile playing at his lips. "Are there any who agree with the rats?"

Not a single paw was raised. Instead, the statement was greeted by laughs.

"Again, are there any who agree with the rats?"

Still no paws.

Silence.

"Really? Not even from the rats?"

All heads turned to the protruding root . . . but Dolley, Moon, and the rat babes were gone.

"Mad?" Lint turned around, but even the black rat had vanished from the branch. "Mad! Where are the rats? Where are they?"

York stepped forward and called down to the defenders, "Don't just stand there! Look for them!"

A few minute later, after searching the rats' burrow, Pib approached the elders and reported his findings. "There is a trail leading from the rats' burrow to the field. It appears they were dragging something."

"Was it the medical supplies?"

"No. Those were untouched. It looks like they dug up something in their burrow. Something they were hiding."

"Corn," said Lint. "They must have kept an emergency storage. Sneaky creatures."

"Should I send defenders to follow the trail and retrieve the corn?" asked Pib.

York shook his head. "No need. With what we took from the rats' burrow earlier, we have plenty of corn to last us many moons. I have a feeling they won't be returning."

"Good riddance, I say," Lint muttered. "Generocity is better off without them and their wretched deeds."

But Lint was wrong. The rats *had* committed one last deed before their hasty departure.

The next morning, Humphrey's corpse lay in the rehabilitation room within the cottonwood tree, his furry throat slit from ear to ear. Found at the scene was a shard of glass wrapped with a makeshift cloth handle. On the wall was carved a single word: *Justice.*

Generocity wept as they buried Humphrey's remains. He had been a poor, confused mouse, unable to control his actions, killed by a psychotic rat.

Chapter 29

How to Find Happiness

"**E**nding my Mate Vow with Pearl was the best thing I've ever done," said Twig behind Benny's back.

Benny was only partially listening, trying to clean a gash on the back of a field-mouse's skull. His dull claws made it an awkward task.

Since the Generocitians had filed their claws, Benny had noticed a strong decrease in claw wounds. Injuries caused by fangs, however, had increased dramatically.

"I don't think Pearl and I ever loved each other."

Benny leaned back, examining the wound, and placed the bandages in Twig's paw. "Did you see how I wrapped the last wound?"

"What? Oh yeah," Twig lied.

Benny sighed. So far, the fat mouse was more of a hindrance than a help.

Earlier that morning, Twig had approached Benny, asking to learn healing. Benny had happily agreed to train Twig for a payment of five kernels.

Twig grumbled at the amount and left the burrow. Benny supposed it was to go work in the field for the kernels. Only a short while later, Twig reappeared with the elder mice at his side, including Benny's father.

"Benny, what is this I hear about you charging Twig to learn?"

"It was just five kernels. Nothing what the rats charged—"

"Benny, what did I say just a few nights ago? Each mouse only gets ten pieces of corn a day."

"Then why would I want to teach Twig?"

York frowned. "Benny, you should be wanting to teach Twig because it is what's best for Generocity. I did not raise a mouse to think of himself. Now, teach Twig."

And that was how Twig became Benny's apprentice.

Benny sighed as the fat mouse created a bundled mess of gauze around the patient's head. The poor field-mouse could barely breathe. Twig had his mind on other things. "It was a mistake making a Mate Vow to Pearl. I guess I'm to blame there. But she was always—"

"Here, move," Benny commanded, pushing Twig to the side and undoing the bandage, allowing the field-mouse to gasp for breath. "I just showed you how to do this on the last patient? Weren't you paying attention?"

Twig just shrugged. "Meh."

"You're not even trying! It's going to take weeks till you learn how to do this."

But Twig dismissed the comment and, instead, continued talking about his ex-mate. "And she never wanted me to be happy. I never had any time to myself. It was always about her and the babes."

Something about Twig's words scratched at Benny's conscience. "But are you sure it was the right thing to do?" asked Benny, not turning from his work.

"What do you mean?"

"Well, isn't that the point of a Mate Vow? To not break it no matter what?"

"Why can't I break it?" asked Twig.

"Well, because . . . because it's not right," Benny sputtered.

"How is it not right? It's just a tradition?" Twig began to raise his voice. "I'm happier, aren't I? Why would it be wrong?"

"Because it goes against the . . ." But the words died in the young mouse's throat.

Twig had caught on. "What? The Old Code? Pssh! You actually listened to that rat dung? Females, whiskey, and food. That's happiness. That's my code."

"That's not what I meant!" Benny said defensively. "No, I don't believe in The Old Code . . . I mean . . . it's just . . . just . . ." But Benny gave up with a sigh. "You're right, Twig. There's nothing wrong with ending your Mate Vow. I'm glad you're happy."

Benny finished wrapping his patient's head. The field-mouse, indifferent to the cost, for the corn had come from the Kindness Pile, handed over to Benny a full leaf.

Twig's eyes bulged, seeing the amount. He licked his lips. "So do I get half of that?"

Benny looked at Twig, puzzled. "Don't you remember what my father said? All corn earned goes to the Kindness Pile."

"So we don't get to keep any of it?"

Benny sighed. "No. We'll drop it off at the end of the day when I collect my ten kernels."

"Wait. So why are we wasting our time being healers?"

"Because . . . because it's the right thing," replied Benny. "Because we are proud citizens of Generocity."

Twig did not seem satisfied by the answer.

Benny wasn't either.

The next day, Twig did not show up to learn.

Benny, free of any patients (very rare), decided to head out into the field to harvest. On his way, Benny caught sight of Twig watching a game of Burrow Rush, sipping whiskey from a seed shell.

"Why didn't you show up? I'm supposed to teach you," Benny asked.

Twig shrugged, not tearing his eyes from the game. "I just got tired of it. I mean, what is the point of all that work?"

"But don't you want to earn lots of—" But Benny stopped himself. That's right, every mouse only made ten kernels a day. "Well, are you going to go harvest, then?"

"Why?"

"Well, so you don't starve?"

"I won't."

"How?"

But at that moment, the team Twig had been rooting for scored the winning goal, and the fat mouse threw his drink in the air and shouted with joy.

Benny, confused, walked into the field. Stud was the only mouse there.

"Where is everybody?" asked Benny.

"Don't know. Oats came earlier, but complained of a hurt paw and left. Said he couldn't bear the pain. I didn't see a wound. I thought you would be teaching Fatty how to heal?"

"Twig doesn't want to be a healer anymore."

"Really? Why not? He used to be all excited about the idea. Getting piles of corn just for helping . . ." But Stud's voice trailed off when the answer came to him just as it had to Benny. "Oh."

Stud went back to ripping off the husk with his teeth. Benny joined him in harvesting. After a while, Stud broke the silence. "Honestly, I haven't noticed much of a difference after we started contributing all we earned; before the change, I was contributing so much of my corn at the end of the day, I only had a few kernels left anyways."

Benny nodded. "I guess."

"And who cares about corn? Right? That's greedy. Just like the rats. I mean, the best part of this is that we are helping Generocity. Adding to the pile. We're doing good, right?"

Benny peered around at the cornfield, absent of workers. In the distance came cheers and laughter.

"Yeah, Stud. We're . . . we're doing good."

Stud and Benny trudged to the Kindness Pile with their leaves. They were drenched in sweat, exhausted. Benny remembered a time when he had felt proud of the sweat and blistered paws. But as the two defenders pulled away his leaf and dumped the corn into the top of the beer can, the pride was gone.

As the defenders were emptying Stud's leaf, who did his best to hold his head high, a group of mice approached. Many of the mice Benny had seen playing Burrow Rush earlier. Twig was with them.

Without even having to ask, a defender opened the metal flap at the bottom of the can and counted out ten kernels for each of the mice.

"But they didn't even do anything today!" cried out Stud.

The defenders and the mice were aghast.

"But we're hungry," said one with a pained expression.

"You don't want us to starve, do you?"

"Well, no." said Stud.

A defender mouse shoved Stud and Benny to the back of the group. "Then get in line for your corn like the rest of 'em."

Chapter 30

A Teacher's Plea

At dusk, Hazel had not been dropped off at the burrow. Concerned for his sister, Benny went to the cinderblock.

As Benny approached the CLAS area, he heard shouts and screams. He picked up his pace, which turned into a sprint as horrible possibilities came to his mind.

Indeed the scene was pure pandemonium. Multiple groups of babes were in fights. The younger ones were crying for their mothers and fathers, covered in dirt and mud. As Benny was catching his breath, a babe ran up and bit Benny on the hind leg before giggling and running off.

"Hazel!" Benny called. "Hazel! Have any of you seen Hazel?" A babe ran by, and Benny grabbed its tail. "Have you seen Hazel?"

The babe, foaming at the mouth, shouted, "Like I would tell you!" and spat in Benny's face. Any babe not busy crying, fighting, or screaming, pointed and laughed as Benny wiped the saliva off.

"Benny? Is that you?" It was Pebble. She was covered in cuts and bruises. Her fur was tousled and her eyes red, evidence of crying.

"What's going on here?" asked Benny. "Why are they acting like this?"

"It's been like this for the past few days, and their behavior is only getting worse. Oh, watch out for Sunshine. She likes to throw"—suddenly, Pebble grabbed Benny's shoulder and pulled him down. Something whizzed by where Benny's face had just been—"rocks."

"Shouldn't they be, I don't know . . . learning something?"

Pebble burst into laughter. "Teach them? I'll be happy if I just get to my burrow alive by the end of the day."

"Why don't you do something?"

"Like what? I tried rewarding them with treats, but they either wanted more or just didn't care."

"Couldn't you just send them home?"

"I can't. The elders won't let me. It's the opposite. They want me to give the ones who misbehave more attention."

"Doesn't that hurt the education of the good babes?"

"What do you think? Besides, the last time I sent a babe home, I had a mother down my throat. She screamed I can't send her babe home, and if they are misbehaving, it's all my fault. My fault? I only wanted to teach, Benny. I only wanted to teach! Not raise babes!" she wailed.

Benny waited for her to wipe her snout before asking, "But it's so late. Why are they here now? Why wasn't Hazel dropped off?"

"Timber, the mouse in charge, said it was too stressful and quit yesterday, and I haven't been able to find a replacement. I . . . I've . . ." Pebble's tears began anew, and she lost her composure. "Oh Benny, I don't know what to do! I've asked everyone—anyone to help me teach or to drop the babes off at their burrows, but no one will. Why would they? They get just as much corn doing nothing! So I've just been waiting here until parents come to pick them up and . . . and it's been hours, and you're the only one who's showed up so far."

Benny put a paw around Pebble and led her away from the madness. "Calm down, Pebble. Just calm down. What about your mate? Is he able to help? Does he know you're still here?"

"Mate? Oh, Benny, I don't have a mate anymore. I ended that foolish vow days ago."

Benny's mouth dropped. "But why?"

"Why? Why not! We weren't happy anymo—*ahh!*"

Hazel, at that moment, had made herself known by sneaking up and jabbing Pebble in the rear with a stick.

Benny ripped the stick from his sister's paw. "Come on, Hazel, we're going home."

Hazel hissed and tried biting his tail.

"Ow! Stop it, Hazel. What's going on with you?"

"Oh no!" begged Pebble. "Please don't leave me here alone. Not with them."

Benny yanked on his sister's paw, pulling her away from the pitiful teacher. "Don't worry, Pebble," he called over his shoulder. "No parents are that bad. They'll show up eventually."

"But what should I do?" she yelled back. "How do I make them behave? I don't know what to do!"

Benny, not knowing the answer himself, just kept walking.

Benny was awoken by a kick to his backside.

It was his father. He tottered from side to side. "Why isn't she at CLAS!" he shouted down at Benny, pointing to the corner where Hazel was hissing, her eyes wild. York's breath had the stench of whiskey. He was drunk.

"Timber . . . Timber quit and Pebble couldn't find anyone to pick her up," Benny explained, rubbing his rear.

"And so you are just going to let her stay here?"

"I . . . I didn't think it was safe for her to—"

York kicked Benny again.

"Father, stop that!" he cried. "It hurts!"

But York continued shouting in a rage, drool dripping down his mouth. "Safe? She's starving! It's not our job to feed her! All of our corn goes to the Kindness Pile, you stupid brat! She is supposed to get her meals from CLAS!" He kicked Benny again, blowing the air from his stomach. "I shouldn't have to come home to that rebellious little monster!"

"But . . . but, Father, you didn't see what was—" Another kick sent him into a whimper.

"Now get up and get her to CLAS!"

Seeing York prep another kick, Benny scrambled to his feet and pulled his sister from the corner.

"And when you come back tonight, bring me your ten kernels from the Kindness Pile."

"But where are yours? Those are my ten kernels. What will I—"

York hissed and lunged to snap on Benny's tail. Fortunately, York was so drunk he tripped over his own tail and stumbled into the dirt wall. "You do what your father tells you!" he said while coughing on dust.

Not waiting for his father to find his balance, Benny pushed Hazel out of the hole into the cool morning air.

From back in the burrow, he heard his father muttering to himself. "Benny, Benny, Benny! Always thinking about yourself . . . dung, I need a drink . . . Cookie will let me borrow . . . yes, Cookie will share a drink."

While Benny and his sister plowed through the crumpled dead leaves of the cottonwood towards the cinderblock, there came a strange rumble from the direction of the field. Hazel ceased her incessant hissing and biting, and both mice's ears perked up.

Benny shrugged. "It's probably just thunder," he muttered to himself.

At the cinderblock, Pebble was not in sight. Babes were scattered, some huddled in groups and sleeping.

Surely the babes had not been left there all night? Surely their parents had come? Maybe the babes had just been dropped off early? Yeah, that was it, Benny convinced himself. The parents had dropped these babes off early.

Benny stood by the cinderblock for a few more minutes.

"It is really early in the morning," Benny said to his sister. "I'm sure your teacher will show up eventually. I have to go now and—*ow!*"

Hazel bit his paw and scurried off towards the cinderblock.

Benny licked the wound and muttered, "Brat."

Chapter 31

The Green Monster

As Benny harvested, the rumble of the strange thunder only continued to grow louder, yet the sky still showed no hint of a visible storm. It wasn't until Benny sat down on a half-harvested ear of corn to rest that he noticed the stones vibrated and danced upon the dirt by his feet. He peered around and saw the leaves of the cornstalks shaking, yet there was no breeze.

Stranger still, where were the mice? Why was he the only one? Where was Stud? Usually, he was out here by now, harvesting.

Benny knew why. These were stupid questions. Could he blame Stud? Could he blame any of them? Why would you want to work for a little when doing nothing earned just as much? There was corn, right over there in the Kindness Pile.

"I'm a bigger fool than them," said Benny out loud. He stood, his mind made up. He would never harvest another piece of corn as long as he lived. He wanted to drink whiskey, sleep, and maybe even find a pretty female. Female? Females! Why not?

The rumble turned into a roar. Benny, deep in thought, did not notice.

What about healing? Benny shivered at the thought of the long line of patients, the complaining, the blood, and the stress. If he couldn't earn large amounts of corn, it was all pointless. No, he was done with healing. There would always be mice who—

An ear of corn fell from the sky, shaken loose by the vibrations. Benny snapped awake from his thoughts. The roar was deafening. In fact, it seemed to be coming from right behind . . .

As the small mouse turned his black head, he was confronted by a large monster with green metallic skin. It was as tall as a tree and devoured the rows of corn. Large, strangely shaped teeth were ripping and shredding everything before Benny's eyes as the monster headed straight towards him.

Benny broke from his frozen trance and scampered out of the way, dodging falling husks and coughing on dust. The creature lumbered past and continued on, leaving a path of shattered stalks in its wake.

Benny stood and looked around, horrified. He was part of a decimated landscape, stretching to the horizon from where the monster had come. The cornstalks behind its path jabbed up into the morning sky like a forest of broken fingers.

He needed to find help! Benny ran through the small strip of unharvested corn, through the clearing, and into Generocity near the cottonwood tree. He had half expected to see mice running in panic at the sight of the monster's head poking above the remaining uneaten cornstalks, and for there to be squeaking and crying, but instead, there was only silence.

"It's eating all the corn! It's eating all the corn!" Benny cried, but no one came to his aid.

The rumbling of the creature had grown faint as it traveled away. Benny placed a paw over his eyes and squinted. The creature began to turn, starting its final pass.

It was not until Benny arrived at the whiskey bottle in the center of Generocity that he discovered many of Generocity's citizens, still passed out from the night's activities. Benny found his father at the base of the whiskey bottle, asleep.

"Father! Father! A monster! There's a monster, and it's eating all the corn!"

York gave a groan and rubbed his eyes. "Oh . . . oh, Benny? What . . . what time is it?"

"Father! There's a monster eating all the corn!"

York's eyes shot open, and they darted back and forth. "A monster? What do you mean? Is . . . is it attacking us? Is Generocity under attack?"

"No, I don't think so. It didn't try eating me. I think it only wants the corn."

The tension in York's body dissipated. He released a long breath and placed a paw on his chest. "Are you sure it only wants the corn?"

Benny nodded.

The rumbling of the creature began to crescendo once more.

York frowned and closed his eyes and turned over on his side. "Well, as long as it is only eating the corn . . ."

"Wait. Aren't you going to do something? The . . . the corn."

"Benny, if we need corn, we'll get it from the Kindness Pile. Now, go away and let me get some sleep. That whiskey isn't sitting right."

Not knowing what else to do, Benny trudged to the edge of the field. There, he sat and waited. A few moments later, the monster's black wheels rolled by on its final pass. It ate the last patch of corn, turned, and rumbled away.

Benny, still sitting, watched as it disappeared into the distance, and still he sat. He sat there all through the morning and all through the afternoon as the flies began to buzz around him. He sat there as the sky turned the color of blood.

When the edge of the sun slithered away, the faint glow of the full moon took its place.

The moon.

"Moon," Benny muttered.

If she was here, she would know what to do. The rats always knew what to do. Just like how the rats had saved them from the humans, or how they had saved Hazel when she—

"Hazel!" Benny shouted and then leapt to his paws, scampering off to the cinderblock. Drowning in his despair, he had completely forgotten her.

There came a sharp, cold, breeze, biting at the fur on his back. Benny shivered.

Chapter 32

The Leftovers

The babes ran amuck, fighting and shouting in the darkness. Others lay huddled in groups, trying desperately to stay warm through the cold night. Here and there came a pitiful cough. Slowly, the babes took notice of the adult wandering through their midst. One by one they ceased what they were doing and approached Benny.

One babe, especially small, tugged at Benny's tail. "Do . . . do you have food? Hungry. I'm hungry."

Benny shook the mouse off his tail. "No, I'm sorry, but . . ."

More paws, outstretched, clutched at Benny's fur. "Food! Please, we need food!"

"I don't have any corn! Get off!" Benny shouted. "Hazel! Where are you—I'm sorry. I don't have any corn—Hazel!"

"Corn! We want corn!" they shouted back.

A paw grabbed Benny's hind foot.

"I said I don't have any corn!" Benny turned and, with the back of his paw, struck down the babe clinging to his foot.

The babe fell back with a bloody snout. It was Hazel.

The crowd, fearing the same consequence, dispersed, hissing at the stranger as they slunk away.

"Oh . . . oh, Hazel." Benny lifted her up. "I didn't know. Come on. I've got to get you out of here."

Suddenly, there was laughter. Benny turned and saw two figures approaching the cinderblock. One was a female, holding something in her paws, and the other was the fat mouse, Twig. The female gave a surprised shout as Twig swatted her rump playfully, and then the two burst into giggles.

"So, Beautiful, what are you planning on doing with that thing?"

"This?" She was disgusted by the object in her paws. "Just a leftover from my last lover."

Twig peered at the thing in her paws. "Why does it look like that?"

"The rats said I shouldn't have been drinking whiskey. What do they know?"

"Aren't you going to take care of it?"

"Why? And by myself? Besides, it's my life, and I can do whatever I want," she said with a huff. "That's what is so great about Generocity: freedom. Anyways, it's not my responsibility to take care of it. That's what CLAS and the Kindness Pile are for."

The female dropped the "thing" into the dirt, where it landed with a plop.

It cried out.

"But I can collect an extra ten pieces of corn now. Wanna go get a drink? I'm paying." The two turned and walked away, not even glancing back. "My life would be miserable if I couldn't drink or," she said, rubbing a paw through Twig's fur, "enjoy the company of a male."

"How about we get that drink later?" said Twig. "I'm thirsty for . . . other things."

The couple's laughter drowned out the "thing's" weeping at the base of the cinderblock

Benny looked down at his sister. Her ribs had begun to show.

"Come on, Hazel. Let's go get some food."

Chapter 33

Impossible

Benny approached the beer can. A defender sat at the base asleep, his back resting against the aluminum. Benny nudged him awake with his foot. "I'm here to collect my corn for the day."

The defender stood up, grumbling. He lifted the hinged flap at the bottom of the can and reached inside with one paw. Benny saw the defender's long, sharpened claws glisten in the moonlight. Benny rubbed his own dull claws together, envious . . . and feeling a bit vulnerable.

"Ah," the defender muttered and pulled out one kernel. "There's one." The defender reached back inside the can and continued to feel around.

The defender frowned and patted around some more. The frown transformed into a worried expression. "Hold on," muttered the defender. He lifted up a stick and leaned it against the top of the can. The defender scampered up the stick ladder and looked down inside. His whiskers drooped.

"What is it?" Benny asked.

The mouse did not reply.

"What's wrong?" Benny asked again.

The mouse shook his head and began to climb down. "Oh its noth—" The defender's footing slipped, and the mouse, catching himself, grabbed the top of the can as the stick fell over. The defender dangled, his feet dancing in midair. Slowly, the can began to tilt and fall in the direction of Benny and Hazel. The two scampered back as the can fell on its side, along with the defender. The defender stood up, groaning in pain, but Benny paid him no heed.

He was staring into the inside of the can.

"It can't be empty! That's impossible," said York. "After we put the rats' corn in there, it was overflowing. You said it would last us months!" York shoved Cookie against the dirt wall of the burrow and squeezed his furry neck. "It's only been a week! You were in charge to make sure this didn't happen!"

"The . . . the rats must be . . . must be stealing it," Cookie sputtered between gasps of breath.

"The rats?" York released his hold on Cookie. "Stealing?"

Lint hobbled forward with Pib, Fib, and Tib at his sides. "I knew this day would come: when the rats, starving and miserable, would return to torment Generocity. They are covetous creatures. What did you expect, York?"

"But I thought we posted a defender around the Kindness Pile day and night?"

"The rats are sneaky creatures, York. Sneaky indeed," he said.

Benny finally spoke up. "What if it wasn't the rats?"

The five mice looked at Benny as if he had gone insane.

"Well, Benny, where do you think all the corn went?" Lint asked before coughing.

"Maybe it's because we take so much from the Kindness Pile? Maybe, since the rats left, no one is contributing anymore. And really, the rats contributed a lot. At least that's what it seemed to me."

"No one contributing?" Lint asked. "Young 'un, are you saying mice are lazy?"

"No! Well, it's not just that. Maybe we should stop depending on—"

"Benny, keep your mouth shut," York commanded. "You three," he said, pointing to Pib, Fib, and Tib, "double the guard around the Kindness Pile. Sooner or later, it has to fill up."

Chapter 34

False Hope

Days passed. Winter came.

Mice would approach the Kindness Pile, asking if it had been filled.

"No, there is still no corn. Come back tomorrow!"

"But I need food! I'm starving!"

"I've been eating leaves and bark."

"I want some whiskey!"

"I said come back tomorrow!"

And the mice would. And the next day . . . and the next . . . and the next.

But despite the extra guards, not a single kernel of corn appeared.

Chapter 35

Oops

Lint, the old mouse, grew sick from the cold and came to Benny, pleading for medicine, knowing if he did not receive any, he would die.

"I'm sorry, but I can't," replied Benny, pushing off the groveling mouse. "I never finished my education. Only the rats knew how to give antibiotics."

"I'll pay you whatever you want. Anything! Anything!"

And for his remaining days, Lint begged and made false promises of corn and food. He even offered to become Benny's personal slave.

Benny, overwhelmed by pity, gave Lint one of the pills Mad had left behind.

A few minutes later, Lint was dead.

Benny never touched medicine again. As a result, mice began to die of wounds and illnesses the rats had easily remedied for a few leaves of corn.

Chapter 36

Twig Finds Happiness

Benny walked up to Stud, who sat shivering in the snow. There was a crunch as Stud bit off the head of a long dead beetle.

"I'm going to work in the field," Benny firmly declared.

Stud squinted up at Benny, wincing as he chewed. "Bu' the 'orn is 'one." A speck of beetle flew from his mouth and landed in the bright white snow.

"Not all of the corn. When the green monster came, I saw an ear fall off its stalk. There may be some out there."

Stud peered back and forth between the half-eaten beetle in his paw and Benny. With great effort, he took a swallow and stood up, tossing his "meal" over his shoulder. "Let's ask Twig if he wants to help."

They found Twig at the base of the cottonwood tree, staring up into its branches. He had lost a considerable amount of weight.

"Twig, we're going to search the field for corn," Stud announced. "You want to come with us?"

Twig did not respond. Instead, he continued staring up into the naked branches of the tree, as if searching for something.

"Twig, did you hear what I said? We're—"

"What's the point?"

"What's the point? What do you mean 'what's the point'? So we don't starve and die, that's the point," said Stud.

"I thought life was about females, and corn, and drink. But I've had it all, and now . . . now it all feels pointless." Twig turned his attention from the branches to Benny and Stud.

Benny realized something about Twig had changed besides his girth. Like the rest of the mice, his fur was filthy, thinning, and unkempt. His whiskers were crinkled, and his lips cracked and bleeding from the cold, dry wind. But looking into Twig's empty, dull eyes, Benny realized they lacked something. He just couldn't put his paw on it.

"We're all gonna die."

The blunt statement caught Benny and Stud off guard, and the two glanced at each other, not knowing how to respond.

"Pointless," said Twig, shaking his head. "It's all so pointless." Then he began climbing the trunk.

"Twig, where are you going?" Stud called up to him.

Benny nodded to the field. "Come on, Stud," he whispered. "Leave him be. It's already midday, and it looks like it's going to snow again."

The two turned and began trudging towards the field.

They had not gone far when from behind them came the sound of snapping sticks and a sickening thud. Stud and Benny turned to see Twig's contorted body on top of the same protruding root where the rats had sat during the city's gatherings. Twig's tail and paws twitched. Blood trickled from his mouth, down the bark of the root, and pooled in the snow below.

Stud closed his eyes and looked away from the heartbreaking sight and cursed silently. "Oh, dung!"

Benny stared. "W. . . why? Why, Twig?"

A few other mice had seen Twig's suicide, but their own faces held no surprise. A few twitched their whiskers, and others glanced at the corpse for a second before continuing what they were doing: sleeping and starving.

"Come on, Benny," muttered Stud. "Let's get to work. Twig's made his choice."

Chapter 37

A Spark of Hope

They worked.

It took great effort, digging through the snow in search of corn, and on the rare occasion they did find an ear, half was rotten and inedible. The wind blew, and the cold bit at their black noses and the tips of their ears, but they worked.

They worked, and they worked. At the end of the day, when the sun had set, the two had scavenged enough corn for each mouse to fill an entire crumpled, brown cottonwood leaf.

Though their fur and paws were numb with cold, their tiny hearts were warm with hope and pride.

Chapter 38

Sharing and Caring

As Benny and Stud arrived in Generocity, Cookie caught sight of them. "Hey, is that corn? Where did you get that?"

Upon hearing the word "corn," gaunt and desperate faces of mice popped up out of the snow and burrow holes.

"We scavenged it," announced Benny as the mice approached. "There is more out in the field. You just have to look for—"

"Share it!" growled Cookie. "It belongs to the Kindness Pile!"

"What?"

"Share! Share!" came another cry.

"Contribute!"

"Don't be greedy!"

"They're so rich! So rich!"

"Share!"

Stud placed himself in front of his leaf. "Over my dead body. This is my corn!"

Pib, the defender, approached Stud. His thin fur stretched tightly over his ribs. His eyes were wild with starvation. "I haven't eaten for days! I'll kill you!" he squeaked madly.

"You wouldn't dare. You'll be sent to the rehabilitation—"

Pib plunged his razor-sharp claws into Stud's chest.

"The rehabilitation center?" Pib said, finishing Stud's last words. He chuckled as Stud's eyes rolled back in their sockets. "I hope so! At least I'll have food and shelter there."

Stud's body slid off the now-bloody claws and landed face first in the snow. The white beneath his corpse slowly transformed to red.

For a brief moment, only Pib's heavy breathing was heard, and like a wave, the mob washed over the ownerless leaf of corn. There were shouts and squeaks, biting and scratching as they fought madly while Benny and his leaf stood just a few steps away.

Benny realized it didn't matter how hard he worked; he would starve. It didn't matter if he worked in the field tomorrow or the next day: Generocity would force Benny to share himself to death.

Benny grabbed the dried leaf with his teeth and took off.

It was a few seconds before the crowd noticed. "He's taking all of the corn!" shouted Cookie.

Benny ran, dragging the leaf, the occasional kernel falling overboard. The mice of Generocity chased after, their eyes bloodshot and their mouths foaming.

Benny peered behind and saw a majority of the crowd stop to fight for the few pieces of corn fallen from his leaf. Benny scooped up an armful of corn from the leaf and ran on, leaving the rest behind.

It worked. The entire crowd became distracted by the leaf of corn and were so busy fighting and killing each other they forgot about Benny. However, it wouldn't be long till that corn, too, was gone, and they would come hunting for him.

Benny continued to run until his lungs were on fire, and his heart felt like it would burst. He ran up a hill and came to the large cinderblock. However, there was not a babe in sight. Benny stopped and leaned his back against the stone, wheezing and clutching the corn to his chest.

While looking down, catching his breath, he noticed something in the snow. Benny gave it a nudge with his tail, shaking off the snow. It was a babe's paw, attached to the last remains of an arm, where only a few pieces of fur and flesh clung to bone.

Benny, doing his best not to squeak in fright, pressed his back against the stone. Not tearing his eyes from the mutilated paw, he made his way around the cinderblock. Reaching the corner, there came a muffled noise. Benny peeked around to see two small babes with wild fur, hunched over a bloody, unrecognizable carcass.

"This one tastes good, it does," growled one babe.

"Mmmm . . ." replied the other, nodding his head and licking his red-stained paws. "I like it when the adults drop the smaller ones off. They don't fight as much."

Benny backed away in horror and the corn tumbled from his paws. The sound of the corn plopping into the snow caught the attention of the two babes, who snapped their heads around and bared their fangs. Drool mixed with blood dripped from their snouts.

Turning to run, Benny found himself staring at an army of bloody babes who had crept up behind him. They growled and swished their tails.

All at once, they pounced.

Benny closed his eyes, waiting to be torn to shreds, but instead, heard them rush past towards the corn.

As Benny opened his eyes, a certain babe with brown fur and a deep scar on her side ran by.

"Hazel? Hazel!"

She ignored him and released a ferocious hiss as a smaller babe stepped in her path. The smaller babe hissed back.

"Hazel! It's me, your brother!" Benny called out.

Hazel lashed out with her claws at the stomach of the smaller babe. The babe emitted a squeak of pain and fell into the snow.

The smaller ones, knowing they were no match to fight for the corn, attacked the bleeding babe. They ripped and tore away chunks of fur and flesh as their victim's cries became gurgles.

Hazel grabbed one of the kernels and scampered away, disappearing into the night.

Benny called after her. "Hazel, please listen—"

"Benny!"

Benny turned and saw his father approaching the cinderblock, joined also by Fib and Tib.

"Benny, is that you?"

"Father? Father! I just saw Hazel," Benny called back, tears forming in his eyes. "Father, we have to do something about the babes. We have to—"

"Where is the corn, Benny?" York asked again.

"Father, the mice . . . all of the mice are killing each other. You have to stop it!"

"Don't worry, Benny. We will. I'm already gathering the defenders. I have a plan. We heard how you and Stud found corn. Is there more out there?"

"Yes, I think so."

"Good." York turned to the defender, Tib. "Go get the rest of the defenders. Bring any mouse out into the field and put them to work. Young and old."

"What if they resist?" asked Tib.

"Resist? Resist with what?" shouted York. "They have no claws! If they don't work, kill them."

The defender nodded and scurried back to Generocity, leaving York in Fib's protection.

Benny couldn't believe what he was hearing. "Kill . . . kill them?" he whispered to himself. "But we are supposed to be free."

York turned his attention back to his son. "Come, Benny. You could join us. See, I've already grown my claws out. You can do the same. The others will have to listen to us!"

"But who will protect us from the defenders? Who will protect us from Generocity?" The words of Moon echoed in Benny's memory.

Benny backed away from his father and Fib. "The rats were right."

"What? What was that? Rats? Do you know where they are? Is that where you got that corn? Were you lying?"

"Father, Fib, please listen. The rats said this would happen. They were right. We can still fix it. They were—"

"It *is* the rats!" York snarled. "I'll kill them! They have all the corn! Where are they, Benny? Where are the rats?" he continued to yell, making his way towards his son, unaware of the crouched form sneaking up behind him.

"Father . . . wait—"

York grabbed Benny's throat and shoved his son's snout into the snow. "Where are the rats, Benny? Where are they?"

Benny twisted free and, seeing no other choice, chomped down on his father's leg.

York howled and fell back.

Seeing the wounded prey, Hazel pounced upon her father.

"Hazel, no!" Benny squeaked, but it was useless, for Hazel was no longer a kind, quiet mouse. As with the rest of the babes, lacking the love, guidance, and discipline of an adult, and never learning right from wrong, she had turned into a savage animal.

Hazel landed on York's shoulders. Wrapping her tail around his neck, she began clawing at York's face, sending the elder mouse to his knees and shrieking in pain.

Pib grabbed Hazel, but even he struggled to loosen the ferocious babe's hold.

Seeing his only opportunity of escape, Benny scrambled to his paws and took off into the field, a landscape once abundant with corn and promise.

There was a squeak. As Benny looked over his shoulder, he saw his sister retreating into the darkness, her ambush a failure. York was being helped onto his feet, holding his paws against his mutilated face, blinded.

"Benny!" he screamed. "Benny you come back here. You are a Generocitian. In Generocity we are kind and share and . . . and . . . and bring back that corn you . . . you little rat! You hear me, Benny! You're just another greedy, stinkin', slimy rat!"

Chapter 39

Prey of Prey

There began a blizzard.

Benny continued through the night, blinded, stumbling past the broken cornstalks. He walked, and walked, and walked . . .

Suddenly Benny tumbled downwards into darkness. His face was in dirt. Dirt? Not Snow. Dirt!

Shelter. He was safe.

Exhaustion finally overcame the mouse, and Benny slept.

He was hauling a leaf full of something towards the Kindness Pile, and then he began tossing whatever it was into the beer can. Blood poured from the bottom hatch. Benny looked at what he had been hauling in the leaf . . . mutilated limbs and corpses of babes. From behind, the beer can fell forward, and a wave of mouse corpses poured forth and buried him. He couldn't breathe! He couldn't breathe . . .

Benny awoke and found his face being smothered. He coughed, sputtered, and pushed away.

His paws pressed against a wall of fur.

The room echoed with a low growl. Benny followed the direction of the fur wall until he was confronted by a white snout and two beady eyes staring him down.

It was a opossum, and Benny had fallen into its den.

Without turning his gaze, Benny grabbed a fistful of dirt and tossed it into the opossum's eyes. The creature, blinded, hissed and shook its head furiously. Benny ran up the slope. The opossum regained its senses and lunged, snapping at the mouse's tail.

Benny exited the den. He was surrounded by a forest blanketed by fresh snow.

He stuck out like . . . well, like a black mouse in a forest covered by white snow.

There was no where to run. This was it. Benny remembered his siblings and how they had died screaming.

No. Not him. He wouldn't go like a coward.

He turned to face the opossum head on.

The opossum released another loud hiss, spittle flying from its mouth. It gave a whip of its tail and pounced towards Benny.

Benny closed his eyes and lifted up his paws. Oh well, he thought, at least this death was quick.

Suddenly, there was a loud crash of breaking twigs, followed by a loud squeal.

Benny opened one eye.

Then both.

He was alive.

Only a whisker's breadth before him had appeared a large, gaping pit. Benny peered over the edge. Below, the opossum lay on its side, clawing at the air as several sharpened sticks ran through its abdomen.

It had fallen into a trap.

Around the trap, several portions of the ground moved, and seven figures stood up, dusting the snow off their capes which had been their camouflage.

One of the strange figures approached Benny. He or she was just a little taller than Benny, and held a stick which had been sharpened to a point. The figure pulled back the hood, revealing a white, furry face. It was a rat.

"What do we have here? A mouse? Well, thank the Ancients!" the rat exclaimed. "You're lucky that trap held your weight, or it would be you down there. We've been waiting for that opossum to come out of his den since yesterday morning. Guess he just needed a little incentive." The rat extended a paw. "Name's John."

Benny, dumbstruck at seeing the stranger, just stared at it.

"Okaaay," said the rat, retracting the paw. "We can shake later. Let me introduce you to the rest of us." John led Benny away from the edge of the pit and began pointing at each of the other six figures individually, saying their names as they pulled down their hoods.

"That's Thomas."

"Hello."

"George."

"Nice to meet ya."

"Alexander."

"From what I heard, I never thought a mouse would have it in him."

"Martha."

The female rat gave a shy wave.

"Deborah."

"He's a cutie."

"Ignore her," said John, giving Benny a wink. "She even thinks rocks are cute. Ah, and this is my oldest sister—"

"Benny?" the last figure called out, pulling down her hood and rushing forward, embracing the startled black mouse.

"Moon?" Benny whispered. He began to feel very dizzy.

"Wait, you know this mouse?"

"Believe it or not, you do too." she laughed and turned to her siblings. "He helped deliver you! Isn't that right, Benny?"

There was no answer.

"Benny?"

Due to hunger, lack of sleep, and the emotional toll from the past several days, as well as just being chased by a opossum, Benny had fainted.

Chapter 40

Avaritia

Benny woke up in a burrow. He was warm. He hadn't been warm in weeks. He found himself covered by a blanket made from opossum fur. His nose and whiskers twitched as he smelled something delicious.

Benny sat up in the bed and peered around the burrow. The ground was covered with more hides, ranging from opossum, to skunk, to rabbit. On the wall hung a rack of sharpened spears with intricate engravings. There were crude canvases made of leather displaying paintings of rats and their history. A fire burned merrily in the center of the burrow, its smoke exiting through a hole in the ceiling. Over the fire pit a spear impaled a hunk of sizzling meat.

Benny's mouth watered.

"About time you woke up." Dolley entered, closing the leather curtains behind her that insulated the burrow from the cold. "We need to get some food in you. It looks like you haven't eaten in days. Here." She lifted the spear off the fire pit, pulled off the hunk of meat, and held it out.

Benny eyed it hesitantly.

"Come now. It's just cooked opossum."

Benny cautiously took it and gave it a sniff. He had never tasted meat before . . . and cooked? Benny took a nibble, and then a bite. Opossum grease dribbled down his chin. It was heavenly.

Benny attacked the hunk of meat ravenously, and it was not until Benny looked up to belch that he saw another figure had entered the room. It was Mad.

Mad laid a cloak of white fur at the foot of Benny's blanket. "To keep you warm outside."

Benny wiped his mouth with the back of his paw and gazed down. He brushed his paw across the pure white opossum fur. "Thank you."

"It's not a gift," said Mad. "You helped kill the opossum. You earned it. Can you walk?"

Benny nodded. "I think so."

"Good." Mad turned and began walking out of the burrow. "Once you finish eating, meet me outside."

"Wait. Why?"

"It's time we put you to work. How else are you supposed to survive?"

"Already? But, Mad, I just got here. I don't even know where I am!"

Mad laughed as he grabbed his spear leaning against the wall. "Please, Benny, call me Madison."

Madison pulled back the leather curtains. Light poured into the burrow. Benny heard the sound of hammering, cutting, carving, cooking, learning, and laughter. It was the sound of civilization.

"Welcome to Avaritia, Benny. Here, you are on your own. Here, you are finally free."

As Benny stepped out of the rats' burrow and into the snow, he squinted and adjusted the white cloak of fur around his black shoulders. Once his eyes adjusted to the blinding light he saw he was still in a forest. Icicles clung to the branches of ash and birch trees.

The forest floor was alive with movement. Dozens of rats and field-mice ran around completing various chores, carrying chunks of opossum meat, pulling sleds made of bark filled with corn, or gathering twigs.

Rodents stood at crude concession stands where they squeaked out prices for strange objects and tools, like spears, sharpened stones, shovels carved from bark, and fur cloaks.

"For just twenty kernels, keep you and your mate warm during these cold times!"

"Meat! Get your fresh opossum meat! Just now butchered!"

"For only ten fists of meat, the Jobe clan will build you and your family a new burrow to fit a human!"

A straight line of a dozen rat babes and field-mice, led by a single adult female rat, walked past Benny and Mad. The female called back to the babes, "Alright, now don't forget, when we learn how to start fire, what is my number one concern?"

"Safety," the babes shouted in chorus.

"That's exactly right," replied the teacher.

As the class of students walked by, though most were extremely well-behaved, one small field-mouse pointed at Benny and said, "You look funny. You don't look like a field-mouse or a rat to me."

The rat teacher halted the line and called back, "Lily! How rude! Apologize to that mouse."

"Oh, no, it's—" Benny began, but Madison raised a paw and shook his head, signaling Benny not to interfere.

Lily stared at the ground, embarrassed by the attention of her classmates.

"Lily, apologize right now, or I will inform your father."

Without looking up, the field-mouse said, "I'm sorry I said you looked funny."

Madison cleared his throat and nudged Benny.

"What?"

"Say 'you're forgiven.'" whispered Madison.

"Oh! You're forgiven," said Benny.

Satisfied, the rat teacher continued leading the class, as if the interruption had never happened. "Now, when Thunder shows us how to use fire, remember, you will all be allowed to cook only one fist of meat. So if you don't pay attention the first time, and you burn your meat, what's going to happen?"

"We must face the consequences," squeaked back the choir of rodent babes.

At the end of the line, Lily, the field-mouse, looked over her shoulder, casting Benny a final curious glance.

A few moments later, Moon approached, spear in paw. Except for the black circle around her eye, she blended in with the snow perfectly. "Oh, Benny, you're already up. That was fast." She studied him up and down. "Hmm, that cloak looks good on you."

Benny felt his cheeks go warm as he blushed. "Thanks."

"I have to go trade for more firewood," announced Madison. "Moon, I need you to take Benny to see Bloody Jackson. He told me yesterday he was needing another gutter. If Benny's lucky, maybe the position will still be open."

Bloody Jackson? Another gutter? Benny didn't like the sound of this.

"Yes, father," she answered, dipping her head in obedience.

Madison turned to Benny. "This is your one chance, Benny. If you want, you can pay us rent until you get your own burrow dug."

"What if I don't get the job?"

Madison pulled up his hood and gave a chuckle, "Didn't you hear the babes? You'll have to face the consequences." And with that, Madison stomped away through the snow.

When Benny turned back to Moon, she was already walking away. "Well, come on, Benny. I don't have all morning. I'm going on another hunt this afternoon."

Benny caught up, still glancing around, taking in the sights, sounds, and smells. "Did all of this exist when you got here?" Benny asked.

"It would have made life easier, but no," said Moon. "When we crossed the field, we barely had time to harvest a few leaves of corn before the machine ate it all. Afterwards, my father knew if we didn't find food soon, we would starve. We ran into a family of field-mice, and my father proposed, with drawings, we hunt for our food." Here Moon laughed. "You should have seen the looks on the field-mice's faces when he drew a picture of a opossum in the dirt. But like us, they were starving and desperate. We had only our teeth and claws at the time. We thought if we snuck up on the opossum while sleeping, we could take it by surprise."

"And you killed it?" Benny asked.

Moon frowned, "No. It was a disaster. In fact, Lily, the babe who just apologized to you; it was her mother that was killed."

"Oh."

Moon shrugged. "But we discovered a tool. A tool twenty times longer than any fang or claw: spears."

Benny stared at Moon's own spear grasped in her paw. "Who created the first one?"

Moon smiled proudly. "You could say it was an accident. One night, starving, I started chewing on a stick. I noticed how sharp the point was. Then, I came up with this." She nodded to the spear grasped in her paw. "After that, once we killed the opossum, the place just exploded. Field-rats smelled the corpse, and once seeing what we had done, the word spread, and they asked us to teach them. My father agreed, but for a payment, of course. Well, in order to pay my father, the other rats and field-mice had to get creative."

Moon pointed to a field-rat standing next to a fire-pit, speaking to the class of rodent babes. "Thunder snuck into a family's house just to learn how humans start fire. He knew rats and field-mice would pay handsomely to stay warm or to cook their meat. By the way, cooked meat stays good for an extra two moons. You can have that piece of advice for free.

"Anyways, no one knows how to start a fire except for Thunder. He keeps it a secret. If your fire goes out, you have to pay Thunder a huge price in meat before he'll let you grab a burning twig."

"But why doesn't Thunder teach others how to start a fire? Why keep it to himself?"

Moon stopped in her tracks and peered at Benny like he was an idiot. "It's how he earns food, of course. He risked his life to gain that knowledge. If he gave up that secret, how else would he eat? If you want to learn the secret, you are free to sneak into a human's house and watch them days on end like Thunder."

Benny said nothing.

"I didn't think so." Moon continued walking. "With knowledge comes power, and with power comes food. My father always taught me that. So, if you want to learn, you'll have to pay. The better the mentor, the higher the cost. The only thing you can learn for free is The Old Code."

"What happens if I choose not to follow The Old Code? Will I be punished?"

Moon froze, slowly turned and quietly said, "No, you are free to believe what you wish. But if that is your decision, you will have my pity, for such a life is one of pointless existence without hope."

The two stared at each other in silence.

Moon, with a swish of her cloak, turned and continued walking. "Come. We're almost there. The butchery is on the outskirts of Avaritia due to the smell. If Bloody Jackson does give you a job as a gutter, I won't envy you, but it's better than starving."

Chapter 41

Guts

The butchery was stationed next to an oak sapling. The scene, described in the most delicate way, was messy. Very, very messy. There lay several skinned carcasses of opossums, raccoons, and rabbits. Rats and field-mice ran around, soaked in blood, slicing meat from the carcasses and stacking it in piles. Several rodents standing near the sapling hung strips of furs over its branches to allow them to dry. At the same time, a rat with a sharp rock scraped off the extra flesh clinging to the backsides of the hides. A field-mouse and a rat, working together, dragged freshly harvested intestines, livers, and bones to a hillside. On top of the hill were two piles, one consisting of rotting guts, and the other of bones.

The smell, indeed, was horrendous, and even in the cold, flies swarmed everywhere. The snow had soaked up the blood, and the entire work area was red, made even more vibrant as it contrasted against the white snowy background.

As Moon and Benny approached, a rat standing on a opossum's carcass shouted down, "Hey, Jackson, Madison's daughter is here to see you!"

A rat soaked in blood crawled out of an opening in the carcass's abdomen. Shaking his body, opossum blood sprayed every which way, showering workers around him who, also soaked, did not notice. Jackson stood up, wiping his blood-drenched paws fruitlessly on his blood-drenched fur. He reached out, grabbed Benny's paw with a loud *squelch* and gave it a good shake. "By jove! You must be Benny. A pleasure to meet you, Chap." He released, and Benny stared at his paw, now tainted red.

Bloody Jackson turned his attention to Moon. He made a grab for her paw, but she coldly said, "Jackson, I told you, touch me, and they'll start calling you Bloodied-up Jackson."

"Right, my dear. My apologies. My apologies." He backed off and gave Benny a slap on the shoulder, leaving a red paw print on his black fur. "Madison told me you would be stopping by. Well, I guess I'll take it from here, Moon."

"Thanks, Jackson. I'll be back by the end of the day to pick up the hunters' share of the meat," she said, pointing to the large stack of slabs of opossum meat.

"Wait. If that's what the hunters get, what do gutters get in return?" Benny asked.

"Why, Chap, see that pile over there?" Jackson said, pointing to a pile of meat half the size of the hunters'. "That's what we'll split up at the end of the day."

"So the hunters get more food than the gutters? That's kind of greedy."

Suddenly, all activity came to a halt around Benny. Every rat and field-mouse stared at him with stunned expressions.

Moon, who had been in the process of walking away, stopped in her tracks.

Jackson took a step back from Benny and whispered, "Oh, Chap, I wouldn't have said that if I were you."

Moon turned, a flame in her eyes. She threw down her spear and stomped towards Benny. "Yes, Benny, we are greedy. All of us. But does that make us evil? The hunters die by the dozens every month fighting beasts, hoping to earn enough for their families. They take the greatest risk, so they get the higest pay. Does this sound evil? What about the ones who save for times of famine and disaster? Are they evil? And the babes who study till their brains ache, greedy of success? Are they evil? And what of those who, due to their greed, invent tools to make our lives easier? Are they evil as well?"

Benny felt the Avaritians' expectant eyes beat upon his fur, and he cast his own gaze in the red snow in shame.

"What? No?" Moon grabbed Benny's cloak and pulled him close. "Then tell me. What evil deed did my family commit when we risked our lives taking the medical supplies from the human. When we spent sleepless days learning how to heal. Tell me what we did wrong when mice came to us willingly, and for only a few leaves of corn, my father was able to help them escape death, such as your sister, Hazel. Tell me, Benny."

Benny said nothing.

Moon grabbed Benny's black fur around his neck and pulled the mouse so close that their snouts nearly touched. "I said tell me!"

Benny only trembled.

"Taking what you don't earn, *that* is a truly evil greed. If you want proof, go back to Generocity. I'm sure they miss you." With that, Moon released her grip, and Benny collapsed into the red snow, unable to look into her pink eyes.

Moon, now disgusted at herself for losing her temper, trudged away, picking up her spear as she left.

Bloody Jackson extended a paw down to Benny, giving him a sympathetic smile. "Let's work."

Benny grabbed the paw.

Bloody Jackson led him to the opening in the opossum carcass. "Since you're new, you get the fun job of gutting. I will show you once, and then you're on your own. And if you feel like you're going to vomit, please be a gentlemouse, and do it outside. No need in spoiling the meat. Customers wouldn't like that." And then, with a "Tallyho!" Jackson crawled back inside the stomach of the opossum.

Benny, taking a deep breath, did the same.

Jackson showed Benny how to hold the sharpened stone tool, then how to cut and slice the meat.

"And be careful of the bladders. You don't want what's inside of those leaking out on you. Trust me. If you come across any bones, throw 'em in the bone pile next to the guts."

"What do you do with them?"

"The guts and bones? Nothing. But if you're feeling a bit peckish, you know where to find the only free meat in all of Avaritia," said Jackson. Then he added with a wink, "You'll just have to fight the flies and maggots for it."

The scraping and cutting was long and laborious, and Benny doubted he would ever get the smell of blood washed from his fur. However, at the end of the day, the gutters received their pay in meat. The experienced, faster workers received more than the beginners. Though Benny received the smallest portion, he still needed a slab of bark to drag the large amount back to Madison's burrow.

"See you tomorrow, Chap," called out Jackson. "You're quite the gutter. Do the same tomorrow, and I'll raise your pay."

Drenched in blood and all sorts of foulness, Benny headed to Avaritia, occasionally glancing back at the pile of meat, proud.

Before he could eat, Benny was politely asked by Dolley to wash himself down in the creek first. The ice had to be cracked and was freezing, but afterwards he dried himself by the rats' fire in the burrow. Benny handed over a payment of meat to Madison for providing shelter, and then began to devour the rest.

Moon, who sat in a corner sharpening a spear, said without looking up, "You need to bury that meat in snow and save it."

Benny wiped his whiskers with the back of his paw. "Why do I need to save it? There will always be animals to hunt. It's not like I'm going to run out."

Moon released a growl. "Sometimes, Benny, I know rocks that have more brains than you!" She threw down her tools, grabbed her cloak, and stormed out of the burrow.

"What's her problem?"

"She cares about you," said Dolley as she added sticks to the fire.

"What?" asked a stunned Benny. "Moon? Like me? Weren't you listening? Moon can't stand me. She tells me all the time!"

Dolley chuckled. "She won't ever admit it, and she'll never show it, but ever since she first saw you, she's had feelings." The white rat shrugged her shoulders. "Call it a mother's instinct."

"When she first saw me? Wait. Back at the humans' house? When I—"

"—Waved at her. Yes. For days, all she talked about was 'a strange black mouse.' We were going to wait until I had given birth to make our escape, but after seeing you, Moon fought with her father, saying the escape couldn't wait."

"She was afraid I would be fed to the snake."

Dolley gave Benny a smile.

Benny looked towards the burrow entrance in disbelief. "Moon?"

"As for the meat," Dolley began crushing some herbs between two stones, "you need to save it to trade for corn when the harvest comes."

"Why? Cooked meat tastes better than corn."

"Because the corn is easier to keep from rotting. You can save it for when you are too old to work."

Dolley stuck a claw in her mouth. "Hmm, some crushed pine needles should do. Benny, could you—"

Benny was already putting on his cloak. "I'll go gather some."

"Thank you, Benny." Then Dolley called out, "Oh, and Benny."

"Yes?"

Her back was to him as she cooked. "Don't tell Moon about this conversation."

The next day, after Benny gutted a raccoon, Jackson kept his word and increased Benny's portion.

Using the food, Benny hired two rats to dig him a burrow. Next, he purchased fire from Thunder. Fearful of his fire going out, he paid Moon to give him a quick lesson on how to keep his fire burning.

"Always have a stockpile of dry wood, especially in cases of emergency. If a snowstorm comes, and you don't have enough, you'll freeze to death."

Moon caught sight of his smoking nest and ran over and stomped out the embers with her tail. "And for the sake of the Ancients, move your nest back. Dry grass and flames don't mix. You don't want to burn alive in your sleep do you?"

Moon also showed him how to cook. "Here," she said, handing him a hunk of sizzling meat. "Tell me if you like it."

Benny took a small bite and swallowed. "Wow! It's delicious."

A bit of gristle stuck to the fur on his snout.

Moon laughed.

"What?"

She leaned forward and wiped it away with her tail. In the process, the two caught each other's stare and froze.

There was silence.

Benny gave a cough. "Well, I should probably go bury half of this."

"Oh. Um . . . yeah," Moon turned away and jabbed a stick at the fire. "Make sure to leave a marker, like a stone or a twig."

Before Benny reached the exit, he stopped, turned, opened his mouth, paused, closed it, and left.

Chapter 42

Purpose

Benny was in the middle of cutting out a hawk's heart when four hunters, including Moon, appeared from the outskirts of the forest, returning from a hunt. Benny lifted a paw to wave, but Jackson grabbed his wrist and shook his head.

The hunters were bloodied and bruised. Their whiskers drooped and each rodent wore a somber expression. They dragged the corpse of a field-mouse on a bark sled, his face covered by his fur cloak.

"Oh, bloody dung," muttered Jackson. "It was Thorn this time."

"Who's Thorn?"

"Lily's father."

"Wait, Lily? Lily the field-mouse? Didn't she lose her mother?"

"Hmm, afraid so."

As the hunters passed by, Jackson and the rest of the gutters bowed their heads in respect to the fallen Avaritian.

"Be at peace with the Ancients, Thorn," said Jackson.

"With the Ancients," repeated the rest of the gutters.

Benny, however, had his gaze on Moon and said nothing.

Benny washed off in the creek and headed back to his own burrow, dragging his day's pay, looking forward to warming himself by the fire.

As he passed Madison's burrow, he heard muffled shouts. Suddenly, Lily the field-mouse came running out into the cold, sobbing. The field-mouse, blinded by tears, ran into Benny and toppled into the snow. "He can't be dead. I don't want him to be dead," she cried.

Benny sat down in the snow. Hesitantly, he picked up Lily and very gently placed her in his lap. At that moment, Moon also came running out of the burrow, her eyes searching frantically for the babe. Catching sight of the two, she relaxed.

"Shh, little babe, shhh," Benny whispered as he stroked Lily's head and rocked her. She was a tiny thing. "It will be okay. It will be okay. I lost my family too. I know what it is like. It will be okay."

"But . . . but I'll never see them again."

"Oh, Lily." Benny looked up into Moon's eyes. "Yes, you will. One day, with . . . with the Ancients. One day."

The answer seemed to suffice, for Lily said no more and, instead, cried herself to sleep in Benny's arms as Moon watched on.

Benny slowly stood, careful not to wake the babe. "Does she have any other family to stay with?" he whispered to Moon.

Moon shook her head. "We were planning on letting her stay with us, but we don't have a clean nest ready."

Benny nodded. "She can sleep in my nest tonight."

As he carried Lily to his burrow, Moon grabbed Benny's sled of meat and followed behind. Once in the burrow, Benny laid Lily down in his nest, tucking her tail in, just like his own mother had done.

"You know there are others willing to take care of her," whispered Moon. "You don't have to do this."

"I know," he replied, not looking up from the babe.

"You'll have to work harder than ever."

"I know."

"So what are you going to do?"

Benny turned and looked at Moon. "Teach me The Old Code."

Moon paused and gave him a puzzled expression, as if not sure this was the real Benny, but peering deeper into his black eyes, she smiled and nodded. "Okay, Benny. Okay. When?"

"Right now. As much as you know."

The next morning, Benny awoke exhausted. While Moon slept in a corner, Benny fed Lily and bathed her with melted snow.

Seeing Lily shiver, he stopped by a vender and bought her a cloak.

"Taking her to CLAS, are you?" the vendor asked, nodding down to Lily.

"Yes."

"The same one her father sent her to?"

"I was planning on it. Why?"

"My babes are taught by a rat named Sap. He's the best. All of his students leave and start earning more than anyone else. Yes, if you want the best for that little one, take her to Sap. He charges a whisker and a tail, though."

Benny asked where to find this teacher, and the vender pointed in the direction of a burrow.

In the burrow, an elderly mouse was having several of his students read out loud from a human book. Noticing Benny, the rat announced, "Let's stop there. Finish reading the passage and practice your algebra problems on the wall. Don't forget, you have a quiz over Shakespeare tomorrow."

He approached Benny. "How can I help you?"

Benny explained.

Sap gave him his quote.

Benny gulped at the price but agreed. He left Lily in Sap's care, promising her he would return at the end of the day.

As the afternoon wore on, and Benny worked relentlessly as a gutter, he began to worry. Doing the math, he realized, as a gutter, he would never make enough food to take care of Lily. Then, his thoughts moved on to Moon. He thought of how Thorn had died, killed in the hunt. It could have been Moon there, pulled on the sled by her companions, her furry cloak draped over her face. Surely there had to be a way to make hunting opossums and raccoons safer. A way to protect them from the claws and the fangs.

There was a loud clatter as a rat tossed a large bone onto the bone pile.

Suddenly, Benny had an idea.

That evening, Benny picked up Lily and fed her. He led the babe to Moon's burrow and asked the rat to watch over her.

"Where are you going?" Moon asked.

"Back to the butchery. There is something I need to do."

It was late at night and Benny sat at the base of the bone pile. He picked up a bone and scratched at it with a claw (rodents were free to have sharp claws in Avaritia). Benny's claw chipped off on the hardness of the bone, not even leaving a mark. He sighed and was lifting his arm to throw the bone back into the pile in defeat when he caught sight of the stone tool he used to peel and hack the flesh off the carcasses.

Benny picked up the stone, covered in dry blood from the day's work, and rubbed it against the bone rapidly. After a few seconds, he ceased the vigorous rubbing, looked down at a mound of bone dust, and smiled.

For the next week, Benny did not leave his burrow.

Though life went on in Avaritia, Moon grew concerned for Benny. She approached his burrow and called down, but Lily appeared instead. "Benny says to stop shouting and to leave him alone."

"Wait. Why? What is he doing?"

Lily disappeared back into the burrow and reappeared a few seconds later. "Benny says not to worry, he is fine, and to please go away."

Many days later, Benny resurfaced from his hole in the ground. He squinted up at the daylight. Benny's eyes had dark shadows, and his fur was a tangled mess. His paws were torn, bleeding, and swollen. As he traveled towards Moon's dwelling, the rats of Avaritia whispered and pointed.

Moon was in the middle of carving another spear when she looked up and dropped what she was doing. "Benny, by The Old Code, what's happened to you?"

Benny ignored the question and instead motioned with a paw. "Follow me. I want to show you something."

They walked back to his burrow, and he led her inside. In the center of the burrow was a stick about Moon's height inserted deep into the ground. From this stick hung bones carved into plates. These plates were then polished and laced together with black opossum hair. The plates formed the outline of a rat's body. To complete the ensemble, a bone helmet was perched on top of the stick.

Moon slowly approached the strange creation and rubbed her paw across the milky white breastplate, engraved with elaborate details of vines and flowers.

She was speechless, awed by its beauty.

"I remember seeing Older Brother Human read a book with pictures of humans fighting," Benny explained. "They wore this shiny cloth for protection. I couldn't read, so I don't know what—"

"Armor," she said, finishing the statement. "I can't believe it. You actually made armor. With this, hunters will never have to fear for their lives again. Think how much they'll pay. How much I would pay!"

"That was the plan. Tomorrow, I'll start making another to sell.

"What about this one?"

"It's yours, Moon."

"What? Oh, okay, I see. Alright, I'll bite." Moon crossed her paws and tilted her head. "How much meat? I'll pay whatever you ask."

"No, not meat."

"Corn then?"

"No."

"Well, what then?"

Benny fell to one knee, grabbed his tail, and held it outstretched to her with both paws. Many times earlier that morning, he had recited the next statement: "Moon, I know this is going to sound crazy, you being a rat, and I a mouse, but in accordance with The Old Code, I ask you to accept my Mate Vow."

Chapter 43

Pursuit

$\mathbf{F}$or a moment, Moon was quiet.

Feeling uneasy, Benny continued to hold out his tail in his damaged paws, his head bent down. "I'm sorry if it's not enough. I've tried my best. If you give me time, I will—"

At these words, Moon burst into laughter. Benny began to blush in embarrassment, thinking himself a fool.

However, Moon, smiling, reached down and grabbed her own tail. She brought it close to Benny's, and the two tails intertwined, symbolizing the acceptance of the Mate Vow. She whispered softly, brushing his black fur, "Till the end, Benny."

That night, in celebration, the Avaritians roasted opossum meat, ate cooked pastries made from crushed corn, and drank the juice of berries collected in the fall, saved for such an occasion. Some thought a mouse and a rat falling in love was a joke, but Benny and Moon were deaf to such comments.

During the festivities, Madison leaned close to Benny and said, "I never thought in one day I would have a mouse for a son-in-law and a field-mouse for a grandbabe."

"Are you upset?"

"About entrusting my daughter into the care of a hardworking mouse? Of course not! The only thing I'm upset about is not thinking of making bone armor first. So, how did you do it, exactly?"

"If you want, I'll teach you," replied Benny, not tearing his eyes from Moon, who danced with Lily in the center of a ring of rats clapping and stomping their feet.

Madison lifted an eyebrow at Benny's offer.

"But the price would be so much, you'd be paying me back for the rest of your lifetime."

At this, Madison released a deep, stone-grinding laugh and gave Benny a slap on the back that nearly sent the poor mouse head-over-tail.

A few more minutes passed, and Benny noticed Madison's smile had transformed into a troublesome expression.

"What's wrong, Madison?" Benny asked.

Madison looked at Benny. "Do you believe in forgiveness?"

"Of course. Isn't that what The Old Code teaches?"

"What about the humans? Could you forgive them?"

"The humans!" Benny felt the fur on his back stand on end as anger filled him at the mere thought of the nighmarish glass prison. "The humans aren't rats, or mice, or field-mice. They aren't us. They don't deserve forgiveness."

Madison replied with a "Hmm . . ." and turned his attention back to the dancing.

"Why do you ask?"

For a second, Madison said nothing, and Benny supposed that was the end of the conversation, but the rat released a sigh, and placed a paw on Benny's shoulder and said: "One day, Avaritia will be faced with a decision. And I fear neither you," he nodded to the crowd, "nor Avaritia will ever be ready."

The song had ended, and the dancers applauded the choir of singers.

"Decision? What decision?"

But as a new tune began, Moon yanked Benny from the outer rim of observers. "Come dance with me!" she squeaked, laughing.

As the crowd cheered on, it was not long till Benny lost himself in the dance with his mate, and had forgotten Madison's strange comment.

Fearing his family's wellbeing, Benny worked harder than ever to craft and sell bone armor to the hunters. His paws soon formed calluses from the repetitive labor of rubbing stone against bone. He also discovered new uses with the bone. For instance, when he strung smaller bits of bone together, he created beautiful necklaces females found enchanting.

Benny began to have so many demands for bone armor and jewelry, he hired several rats and a field-mouse to assist him. By the end of the winter, Benny had gone from being the poorest mouse in Avaritia to the wealthiest.

Each night before bed, Moon and Benny would tuck Lily into her nesting and tell her the ways of The Old Code: how it was wrong to steal, lie, murder, ignore parents, be lazy, and to break a Mate Vow.

Each time the babe did something wrong, Moon or Benny would nip Lily on the tail. It brought the babe to tears, but rarely did Lily repeat the behavior. Never once did Benny bite his babe's tail in hate or anger, but because he loved Lily and did not wish her to become like the babes of Generocity. Despite their mountains of corn, spacious burrow, and piles of furs, Lily was their greatest blessing.

Benny arrived at his burrow late one night, exhausted from the day's labors. However, when Lily leapt into his paws, and Moon approached his side, giving him a welcome-home lick, Benny realized something.

He was happy.

Chapter 44

Home Sweet . . . Never Mind

On a spring morning, when Benny was busy helping a customer, Lily sliced her paw while playing with one of Benny's sharpened stones.

A few days later, the wound began to ooze green, and the babe grew sick and pale.

As Moon sat by the nesting and dabbed Lily's head with a wet cloth, Madison and Benny stood back in the opposite corner.

"You know what this is, don't you?" The rat whispered.

Benny nodded, remembering his sister Hazel. "Yes. So give her that pill."

"Benny, I—"

"What are you waiting for? Give her the pill."

"Benny will you—"

"I don't care what it costs! Just give her the medi—"

"I don't have it anymore!" Madison shouted.

This statement crushed Benny, and he buried his face into his paws and began to weep. "But you're a healer. You're supposed to have medicine!"

Madison placed a paw on his shoulder. "I'm sorry, Benny. It's all gone. After being chased from Generocity, I had to steal a second batch from the humans. I ran out a few weeks ago, but when I went back to the human's home a third time, they had the medicine locked up. It will be weeks before I can find more . . . maybe even months."

However, Benny had stopped listening after the word *home*, for it was that word that sparked a memory. A memory that provided a solution. A solution which horrified him. As Benny lifted his head, his furry cheeks still wet from tears, he had such a hardened expression of fatherly determination that even Madison stepped back.

"I know where to go," declared Benny.

Benny went alone.

Early spring rain drizzled down from the gray sky. Benny waded through the mud and rows of green corn sprouts. He ate on the go and stopped only to relieve himself. There was no time. The infection in his daughter would spread fast.

As evening approached, the leaves of Generocity's cottonwood poked above the tips of the corn sprouts in front of him. He heard a voice in the distance. At first, he thought it was a voice of distress, but as he drew closer, Benny realized the voice was shouting commands.

"Dig faster, slaves! Faster!"

There was a squeak of pain.

Benny crouched between the sprouts, keeping his head low. There were three mice. One of the mice stood on his hind legs. He was a defender. This was apparent by the frightening length of his claws—longer than Benny's head. This defender stood over a mouse babe curled in a fetal position, whimpering. A small distance away was another mouse covered in grime, digging furiously, splattering mud in all directions.

"Get up you little piece of dung!" shouted the defender, landing a kick on the curled babe's face. There was a sickening crunch as the babe's snout shattered. The mud-splattered mouse dug faster, panting.

"I said dig!" the defender commanded. However, the babe only lay in a crumpled heap, emitting a sound that was a mixture of gurgling and crying.

Suddenly, another defender appeared. It was Pib, one of the red-furred triplets. He too had grown his claws out to an incredible length. "Where are the worms?" he growled to the defender standing over the babe. "We're growing hungry, and I have things to—" He saw the bleeding babe on the ground.

Pib crouched next to the babe, gave him a sniff, and winced with disgust. He sighed, patted the babe's head, then stood and turned to his fellow defender. "Remember what the Prophet said about the slaves?"

"Well, yeah . . . I was just . . . uh . . ."

Pib raised his foot and slammed it down on the back of the babe's head and held it there. The babe's snout sunk into the mud. As the babe twisted and squirmed, fighting for breath, Pib talked very slowly and calmly, eyes focused on the defender. "If you can't get the slaves to find worms to eat until the corn grows, then we have no food. And if we have no food, then we have to sacrifice a slave. Now, if we start running out of slaves, guess who is going to start taking their place?"

"Um, us?" replied the defender.

The suffocating babe clutched at the mud, which oozed from between his dull claws.

"Oh no, not just us. You. You will be first."

The babe's body went limp.

Pib glanced down and dusted off his paws, as if just finished with a difficult chore. "Well, there's dinner for tonight."

Pib grabbed the foot of the babe and dragged the body behind him as one would a leaf of corn. As Pib walked past the other mouse digging in the mud, he stopped, leaned forward, and with his free paw, grabbed the digger's muddy arm and inspected its paw.

Shaking his head, Pib released his hold and continued walking. "And before you eat, dull that slave's claws. You don't want them fighting back, do you?"

The shallow ditch plowed by the babe's corpse made it easy for Benny to trail Pib. There came more shouts of commands and cries of pain. Soon, he reached the clearing of Generocity. It was obvious that the population of Generocity had grown immensely. There weren't hundreds of mice.

There were thousands.

The whole city seemed to consist of mud and fur. Groups of slaves walked to and fro, carrying wriggling worms and chopped worm parts as defenders followed, cutting into them with their sharp claws if they slowed.

Another group of slaves sat in a circle, dulling their claws by rubbing them against stones vigorously as defenders inspected the work.

Pib dragged the corpse through the hellish mud pit that was Generocity to the cottonwood tree. He entered a doorway in its trunk, vanishing from view. Benny frowned. That tree was probably where the medicine was. If Benny could get into the tree without being noticed . . . but how?

While thinking, Benny rubbed his own claws together.

Claws.

Wait. Claws! He had claws! Benny glanced at his paw and gulped, arriving at an insane idea.

Benny placed his spear on the ground and covered it with mud. Such a strange tool would grab attention. Next, he grabbed more mud and rubbed it deep into his fur and across his snout. He needed to be covered in mud. Immersed in mud. He flexed his claws, hunched his shoulders, and gave a practiced snarl. He shrugged. Well, he at least *felt* like a defender.

Benny took a deep breath and stepped out of the covering and into Generocity. As he made his way through the crowd, he shoved and pushed slaves in his way, pretending to be unremorseful. "Ugh . . . get out of my way, you piece of dung!" he shouted, ending the statement with a growl. "I'll eat you myself if you look at me like that again."

So far, so good.

As he made his way to the entrance of the cottonwood tree, Benny took notice of a strange fact: there was not a single female mouse in the crowd.

He was still contemplating this mystery when he passed a group of defenders standing around a branch halfway implanted in the ground. Tied to the branch was the elder mouse, Cookie. His leg was twisted in a contorted angle. He was a pitiful thing, weeping and filthy.

"We . . . we were supposed to be a caring society," he pleaded with the defenders. "It's just a broken leg. It will heal! I'll be okay!"

A defender approached Cookie. It was another one of the triplets, Fib. "Cookie, you can't work anymore. You're useless. How are you to contribute to society?"

"But I can contribute! Ask the Prophet! I can! I can count past ten! Do you know anyone who can do that? I can still contri—"

Cookie's protest turned to a gurgle as Fib, with the flick of his wrist, slit the old mouse's throat.

"Dear Ancients, please get me through this," Benny whispered to himself, speeding up his pace. As he approached the tree, both defenders guarding the entrance covered an eye with a paw and chanted, "Praise the Prophet!"

Having no idea what they were talking about, Benny, copied the motion, covering his own left eye with a paw and repeating back, "Praise the Prophet!"

A large open chamber had been carved into the trunk. It was in this chamber that Benny discovered the missing female mice of Generocity.

Two large defenders bumped into Benny as they exited the chamber, laughing, leaving one terrified female mouse with brown fur and a scarred belly lying crumpled on the floor.

"I don't know why you like that one," said one of the defenders. "She's always a fighter. Been a little savage since she was a babe."

Benny recognized her immediately.

"Hazel!" Benny called out. He scurried over and placed a paw on her filthy, brown fur. Her back was littered with scars. At his touch, Hazel flinched. Benny could not tell if it was out of fear or pain.

Behind Hazel a dozen or so female mice were huddled against a wall of the large chamber, quivering with dread. One glanced over her shoulder, and upon making eye contact with Benny, let out a terrified squeak, "Not me! Not me! I've already been chosen today three times. Please, don't choose me."

"Choose you?" Benny asked, and then it dawned on him. "Oh, oh Ancients, no! I won't . . . I wouldn't . . ."

But the female was no longer listening as she tried to literally dig herself deeper into the mound of female mice. "Not me! Not me!"

"Dear Ancients," Benny whispered as pleas for mercy and death echoed off the chamber's walls. Tears came to his eyes. "Oh, dear Ancients, they've become worse than the humans."

Hazel looked up into Benny's watering eyes. "Wait, you're not like the rest. I've met you . . . Benny? Benny!" She burst into tears at the sight of him and threw herself into his paws and embraced him.

Unfortunately, the moment was only brief. Hazel was ripped from her brother's arms as a defender dragged her away by the tail. "Benny! Run!"

Too late. Benny felt his own feet disappear from beneath him as his own tail was given a strong yank. Benny's jaw hit the wood floor, cracking a tooth.

Fib peered down at him. "See, Pib? I told you I've seen his face before!"

Pib landed a kick across Benny's jaw. Before he blacked out, the last thing Benny saw was Hazel, carving lines in the wood with her dull claws as she screamed his name.

Chapter 45

The Prophet of the New Code

"**H**ello, Son. It's been a while."

That voice. Caring. Kind. Loving. It was his father.

Benny's eyes fluttered open.

"I'm sorry for the rude welcome," York said. Benny followed the voice and saw York standing in the corner of the room. His father's fur had grown white and thin. Clumps had fallen out, revealing patches of pink flesh. His face was hidden in a veil of shadow.

"Go on, Benny. Sit up."

As Benny did, he felt something slide off of his body. He had been covered with furs to fend off the spring chill.

Strange, Benny thought as he ran a paw across a pelt, I've never seen furs like this before.

The burrow was large, with only one entrance where light poured through. By this entrance stood a single, scrawny mouse slave. Wispy, hairy roots protruded from the ceiling above their heads. They were underneath the cottonwood tree.

"I'm so happy you returned, Benny," said York. "So, so happy. I was a fool for chasing you off. I hope you can forgive me. You must be starving." He motioned with his paw, and a slave by the doorway approached Benny. He held out a leaf whereupon sat a piece of fresh, uncooked meat. Benny gave it a sniff. It smelled strange.

"Come now. It's Cookie's final contribution. Surely you would not want to dishonor him."

Cookie's final contribution? Benny caught sight of a clump of tan fur clinging to the meat. Benny turned to the side, fell on his paws, and vomited.

As he wiped his mouth with the back of his paw, Benny heard the thuds of his father's cane. A shadow fell over him, and a paw patted him on the back. "There, there. Just give it time. You'll get used to the taste. Here, give me that. Waste not want not, right?" York chuckled. There was a sickening squish as he bit into the meat. "In 'act, I've 'rown 'uite," he gulped, "mm, excuse me—quite fond of it myself."

As Benny stared down at the vomit on the blankets, he realized why the furs looked so familiar: they were mouse furs!

With a shout, Benny kicked the pelts off and placed his back against the wall. He looked into his father's eyes. Only there was one problem . . . York no longer had eyes, just empty pink sockets where they had been ripped out by Hazel.

York frowned and placed the meat back on the leaf. He motioned the slave to go back to his post.

At the same time, Tib, Fib, and Pib rushed in holding six newborn babes. "Prophet, we have new citizens!"

The pups were still blind and furless, crying for their mothers.

York clapped his paws. "Marvelous. Bring them here. It is time for the Ancients to decide their fate. Hold on, Benny, this will only take a second. Slave! Go fetch me the Bowls of Baptism!"

The slave returned with two seed shells, one holding a thick mixture of mud, and the other blood. Where they'd gotten the blood, Benny was afraid to ask.

The first pup was presented to York. The Defender held the babe upside down by the foot before The Prophet's face. York gave the pup a sniff, placed a paw on its tender belly and then whispered a strange language underneath his breath before shouting, "Defender!"

With the declaration, York dipped a claw into the blood bowl the slave held. Then, after patting the pup until finding its head, York brushed a red streak of blood across its forehead.

The next pup was brought forth. Again, York placed a paw on the belly and muttered the strange words, except this time, York shouted, "Slave!" and placed a dab of mud on its forehead.

The next pup only needed a quick sniff from York before he shouted with disgust, "Female! She will be a comfort-giver." Again, a swipe of mud.

The next received a blood streak. "Defender!"

The next, mud: "Slave!"

York sniffed the last babe and smiled. "The Ancients have told me this one will be a strong defender." He dipped a claw in the blood, but just as he was about to brush the pup's forehead, the pup bit the claw.

York shrieked. He dropped his cane and hopped about sucking on his wounded paw.

Pib, Tib, and Fib rushed forward. "Prophet! Are you hurt?"

York motioned them away. "I'm fine!"

"But the—"

"I said I'm—" Suddenly, York gasped and placed a paw on his head and stared up at the ceiling with those empty sockets. "The Ancients have changed their minds! He will be a rebel! A follower of the blasphemous Old Code! He must be sacrificed! Now, go! Deal with him quickly, before the Ancients rain down their wrath."

The defenders nodded and rushed out of the room with all six babes.

Benny stood, mouth gaping in disbelief of what just happened. "Did . . . did you just sentence a pup to die because it bit you?"

"No, not I." York smiled. "It was the Ancients."

"Ancients? But you don't believe in them. You're making it all up.

You're lying to them?"

"I'm lying? I'm lying!" York squeezed his grip tightly on the knob of his cane and flicked his tongue out, licking his lips. "It's those rats. You found them, didn't you? You think you have them figured out, do you? You really trust them? Honestly, Benny, I thought I raised you better. I'm surprised you haven't figured out *their* lies."

"Lies? What do you mean lies?"

York opened up his arms and motioned around. "Where do you think I got the idea to become the 'Prophet' who created the 'New Code?'" York leaned over and tapped his son's head with a claw, making Benny flinch. "Think! Did the rats ever say where they got their Old Code?"

"What do you mean?" Benny didn't see where his father was going with this. "They got it from the Ancients."

"You saw the Ancients, then? You saw them teach the rats The Old Code?"

"Well, no, but I'm sure the rats' parents saw the Ancients . . . or even their grandparents—"

"Oh, Benny! Do you hear yourself? How could you ever know? How could you ever prove it?"

Benny thought but finally sputtered, defeated, "I . . . I can't."

"I know!" York shouted, elated. "You can't!"

Benny shook his head. "But why? Why would they make it up?"

"Power, Benny. Power," York flicked out his tongue again. "Power gained by false hope and ignorance of the masses."

"The Old Code is not a false hope. The Old Code is the truth."

"Like how the defenders believe my New Code is the truth? You honestly think you're any different from them?" York laughed.

No, Benny thought. Moon would never lie to him. She loved him. "I'll tell them all. I'll tell the defenders what you're doing. How you made up the New Code!"

"And who do you think they will believe, hmm? Benny the traitor who abandoned his kind to live with rats, or the Prophet, whose eyes mysteriously 'vanished' when he saw the Ancients as they handed him the New Code. A prophet who satisfies every one of their desires."

York gave a wheezy laugh and coughed. "No, no, no. What your sister did to me that night became my blessing. My salvation. Now, I get all the food I want, any female I want, live anywhere I want, and with a simple 'Thus said the Ancients.'" York patted Benny until he found his son's shoulder. "Stay here with me, Benny. I'll say you saw the Ancients, too, and that they made you a prophet. We'll just have to take care of those eyes."

This was madness.

"No!" Benny slapped his father's paw away.

"Come now, Benny, it doesn't hurt for long."

"You're a maniac!"

"What?" York scoffed. "You would deny what I offer, comforts that any mouse here would die for, to go back to what? Living with rats and their lies?"

"They aren't lies!" Benny's shout echoed in the room, shaking a few specks of dirt from the ceiling.

The two stood in silence.

"So, loving son of mine, if you're not here to enjoy your father's company, what brings you back to our little utopia?"

"I need the medicine that was given to Hazel."

"What for?" York smiled. "Is one of the rats sick? Are they dying?" York asked, hopeful.

"No."

"Oh. Shame."

"It's for my daughter."

This caught York by surprise. "You . . . you have a daughter. I take it you followed those"—he waved a paw in the air—"pointless Mate Vows."

"Yes."

Benny felt it best not to mention that his daughter was a field-mouse and his mate a rat.

"Hmm . . . I always thought when being told I was a grandmouse it would be in"—a slave's scream echoed throughout the chambers of the tree—"better circumstances. What's her name?"

"Lily."

"Do you love her?"

"Yes."

"Hmm . . ." York turned his back.

Without thinking, Benny blurted out, "Why don't you come with me?"

"What? Leave Generocity? Bah! Don't be stupid."

"No, Really. Why not? I have plenty of food and a large burrow. You could see your granddaughter."

York chuckled. " 'See?' I wish."

"Touch her then. Stroke her fur. Tell her stories, and sing to her like you once did to me. Come with me to live, father. To truly live."

York did not answer.

Benny placed a paw on the elderly mouse's back, causing him to jerk. Such a gesture of kindness had long been forgotten in Generocity. "Father, I was once told that mice look out for each other."

"Hmm, I did say that, didn't I?"

"I am a mouse, but father, I am more than just a mouse."

"Really? And what's that?"

"I'm your son."

Silence.

York took a deep breath and nodded, making up his mind. He called out for his slave, who approached, and York whispered something into his ear. The slave scampered off and returned a short while later with a single chipped antibiotic pill.

York handed the medicine to his son. "Here," he said. He turned his back to Benny and hobbled away towards an empty corner, tapping his cane.

"Father?"

York kept his back turned. "Leave, Benny. Leave and never return to this nightmare."

Chapter 46

A Father's Love

Benny, with pill in paw, ran. He ran out of the burrow, past the female mice who screamed for mercy as they were forced to comfort, past the defenders who devoured the corpse of a mouse pup who bit their Prophet, past the slaves covered in mud and scars as they were beaten, past where Benny had buried his spear, and past the rows of corn sprouts.

Through the night and into the morning he ran. Once Benny reached the outskirts of Avaritia, several rats, including Moon, caught sight of him and rushed to his aid. Benny handed the pill to his mate, ignoring any questions, and fell on all fours, weeping.

"Moon, go give the medicine to Lily!" It was Madison. He approached holding a spear.

She needed no urging and was off in a flash.

Madison turned to the rats. "Give him space. I do not envy the things he has probably seen. Go on, get back to work."

Grumbling, the rats did as they were told, leaving Madison and Benny in peace.

"Come, Benny. We need to get you to the burrow to rest."

He placed a claw underneath Benny's arm, but the mouse shrugged him off. Looking up at Madison with teary eyes, he said, "Was it a lie?"

"Was what a—"

"The Ancients, The Old Code. All of it, Madison! Did you make it up?"

Madison stood quietly. He turned his back to Benny and coldly replied, "I was scared if you knew the truth, you would reject everything you learned."

Benny shook his head in disgust, not wanting to hear anymore. "My father was right. You're just like him!"

Suddenly, Madison bared his teeth, releasing a fearful hiss, and raised his spear.

Benny stepped back. "Madison . . . what are you—"

Madison threw the spear with all of his might. The wooden shaft flew by Benny's face, brushing his whiskers, and disappeared into the cornfield. There came a squeak of pain from behind the green corn sprouts.

"What was that?" asked Benny.

Madison, without answering, walked towards the sprouts and pushed them aside, revealing a defender mouse with long claws and blood-war paint, clutching at the shaft protruding from his abdomen as his paws kicked at the ground.

Hearing the two approach, the defender looked up, blood trickling from his mouth, and began to laugh. "You . . . you didn't get us both."

Madison pulled the shaft from the defender's stomach, causing the laughter to turn into another squeal. Madison pointed the bloody tip at the defender's throat. "Where is he headed? Why did you follow Benny?"

"I have served the Prophet. My reward awaits." The mouse coughed, spraying blood. "He will come . . . and with his army . . . you will be punished for your greed . . . greed and blasphemous ways. Your blood will run in . . . in rivers. Your food will be shared. Your sons will be slaves. And your daughters will be made as—"

The defender's statement abruptly ended as Madison plunged the spear through the mouse's throat and into the ground.

The rat turned to Benny.

Benny shook his head and clenched his paws into fists. "He lied to me. My own father. It was all an act. He never cared about Lily."

The rat's expression softened. He placed both paws on Benny's shoulders and looked down at him. "Do not blame yourself. I knew they would find us eventually." Madison pulled his spear from the corpse and walked towards Avaritia. "Come. It's time," he called to Benny.

Benny followed Madison. "Time for what?"

"To defend against this world's greatest threat. A threat that even humans have faced since the beginning of time. A threat worse than starvation, opossums, or snakes."

"What threat?"

Madison glanced down, and for the first time, Benny saw fear in the old rat's eyes.

"Evil."

Altogether, including any rodent above the age of two moons, there were one hundred and forty-three citizens able to defend Avaritia. The next morning, Moon and her brother, John, went into the field to scout out the enemy. They returned that evening just as the sun had set.

The Avaritians gathered around the two, ceasing tasks of hauling dirt and leaves.

"How many?" Benny asked.

Moon shook her head. "I couldn't even count. They've bred like crazy. If I had to guess, a few thousand, at least."

"It will be a slaughter," Bloody Jackson murmured.

"What about Lily and the rest of the babes?" Moon asked.

"Dolley will watch over them in our burrow during the battle," replied Madison. "If need arises, she will lead them deeper into the forest. As for Lily, she's still too sick . . . Benny, I'm sorry."

Benny went back to dragging his sled of freshly dug dirt. The other rats and field-mice did the same, digging and gathering leaves as fast as they could.

In the distance, they could hear the faint howls and screeches of the bloodthirsty defenders, eager for vengeance upon the selfish, blasphemous rats and mice of Avaritia.

Chapter 47

The Last Contribution

Morning.

Gray.

Rain.

A flash of lightning.

A figure dressed in bone armor, spear at his side, stood at the edge of the forest, facing the cornfield. It was Benny, and he was alone.

Another illuminating flash.

The sprouts of corn quivered and shook. A horde of mice emerged, squeaking and shouting in madness, presenting themselves as a solid wall of soaked fur, claws, fangs, and death.

Their eyes darted back and forth, searching for their formidable foes. A defender pointed to the pitifully small mouse in the distance and shouted, "Is that it? That's what we came all the way out here for?"

The horde burst into laughter.

"Quiet, you fools!" The shout immediately silenced the thousands of savages. A section in the ranks was parted by Tib, Fib, and Pib, allowing York to hobble forward.

"Benny! Benny, I know it's you! I can smell you," York shouted across the field. "Stop this stupidity! Tell us where your food is! Where is this new family and society that you are so willing to die for, hmm?"

Benny shifted uneasily in his armor. His silence gave York his answer.

"Ah, so the cowards ran!" York declared with spread paws.

The horde chuckled.

"Come, Benny. Stop this nonsense. Why don't you come back? You could live a life of no fear, no work, and"—York licked his lips—"all pleasure."

The horde cheered and shook their fists in the air.

"No!" Benny shouted back. "My brethren, don't you see what has happened to you? You live off the pain of others. You drink and sleep with whomever you wish. You only care about yourselves and immediate gratification. You live in ignorance, following an insane mouse who has created a twisted truth and calls himself the 'Prophet of the Ancients'! Where is your guilt? Where are the mice who once were loving and kind?"

The savages covered their ears and shouted in shrieks, "Blasphemy! Blasphemy!"

York bellowed, "And so you listen to the rats and their lies!"

"Is The Old Code a lie? I don't know anymore. But then again, does anyone know the *true* truth? Why what happens, happens?" Benny shrugged. "I guess I'll just keep searching. I have to."

All heads in the horde turned to see York's reaction to these words. The old mouse calmly slapped a gnat on his shoulder and rolled the dead thing between his claws. "Only an insolent fool would believe such an idea." The Prophet flicked away the insect's corpse and ordered, "Kill the blasphemer!"

The army charged across the dirt field, trampling the corn sprouts and each other, desiring to rip apart the mouse named Benny.

Even at the sight of this charge, Benny did not falter.

The defenders crossed onto the grassy plain between the cornfield and the forest of Avaritia. They were so close that Benny saw the blacks of their eyes.

Still, Benny did not falter.

The defenders were now only a stone's throw away. They were in such bloodlust, in such a maddened rage, they didn't even notice the floor of leaves stretched in front of Benny, somewhat out of place on the grassy plain between the field and trees.

The first row of blood-painted mice tensed their legs in preparation to pounce on their prey and . . . they vanished from sight. As did the row of mice following them, and the row after that. Each plummeted through the leaves which had, like the traps used to catch opossums, disguised a deep pit filled with sharpened stakes three times taller than Benny.

In seconds, this pit began to fill with blood, writhing bodies, and screams of agony. The defenders continued to topple down to their deaths, for no mouse in the horde could see what was before them until it was too late.

It was not until half the horde had vanished from sight, that the savages realized what was happening and ceased their charge.

Before the mice of Generocity could plan their next move, hundreds of figures clad in fierce bone armor emerged from the ground behind the horde's rear flank, shaking off the mud and grass they had hidden under silently.

It was the Avaritians.

The Avaritians charged forward with their spears. The defenders, seeing the frightful charge of armored rodents, stumbled backwards and more plunged down onto the spikes of the pit.

The Avaritians collided with the defenders of Generocity and impaled them, some even two at a time with their spears. The defenders tried to fight back, but their sharp claws grazed harmlessly against the bone armor.

Although still outnumbered, each rodent of Avaritia fought with more fury than a hundred defenders, for the defenders had only come for food and the pleasure of violence, while the Avaritians fought for their families, their Old Code, and their freedom.

Benny spotted Moon in the fray on the other side of the trench. Five defenders surrounded her, but she appeared surprisingly calm.

"Moon!" Benny shouted and scurried around the deadly trench, fearing for his mate's life. However, as he arrived at the scene, four of the defenders already lay dead at her feet. As Moon was bringing down her spear to end the life of the fifth, a sixth defender emerged from the chaos, attacking her from behind.

Benny recognized he would not reach her in time and threw his spear. Just as Moon turned to face her ambusher, Benny's spear slammed into the spine of the defender, sending him face first into the mud.

Seeing who her savior was, Moon smiled, but her gaze drifted over Benny's shoulder, and her eyes widened in horror. "Benny!" She lifted her spear and pointed to the other side of the trench from where Benny had just been only moments ago.

Pib was carrying York on his shoulders while Tib and Fib followed behind. They had circled around the battlefield, as well as the trench, now with no obstacles between them and Avaritia.

"The babes!" Moon shouted. "They smell the babes!"

Benny and Moon took off. They were making their way around the trench when a defender tackled Benny, hissing and scratching at his armor.

Moon pulled the mouse off her mate and held the hissing creature down with the shaft of her spear. "Go!" she shouted to Benny.

Benny hesitated.

"Benny! Our daughter!"

Lily's weak form flashed through his mind, and Benny, praying to the Ancients to keep Moon safe, ran towards Avaritia, following the muddy paw prints of the three mice.

The sounds of battle faded, leaving Benny in an eerie silence as he ran through the trees.

He came to the end of the trail, and Benny's fears were confirmed as the paw prints disappeared down into Madison and Dolley's burrow.

As Benny rushed inside, he caught sight of Dolley's form lying on the ground and his heart dropped.

Not breathing. Unmoving.

"No."

His whispered cry caught the attention of the four mice surrounding the whimpering babes in the corner. York turned around, holding Lily upside down by her footpaw. "Ah, Benny, I thought I smelled a traitor." The blind mouse lifted up the field-mouse before Benny. "I thought I would come down and visit my grandbabe. She must be yours. She is the only one reeking of illness."

"Release her!"

"Oh, Benny, that is no way to speak to your father. And in front of your daughter? What kind of example are you setting?" He took a sniff of Lily, and a look of disdain crossed his face. "A field-mouse?"

"I said let her go!" Benny gripped his bloody spear tighter.

"Honestly, Benny, I never thought you had it in you. And with a field-mouse?"

"Moon."

"Excuse me?"

"Her mother is Moon. She is my mate."

For a second, York's expression showed no emotion. Then, a barking laugh erupted from his throat. "Well, then you should consider yourself lucky." York nodded to Dolley's corpse. "You never have to worry about a nagging mother-in-law." York burst into laughter again, and the three defenders joined in chorus.

Busy in their mockery, neither noticed Lily reaching for York's swishing tail.

Pib pointed to Benny, "Oi! Look at that. He's going to cry. I think he loved that rat!"

The four screeching howls of laughter grew louder as tears watered in Benny's eyes. The black mouse gritted his teeth and muttered something.

York quieted them. "What was that?"

Lily caught York's tail.

"I did love her!"

The babe bit with all her might.

York shrieked, dropping Lily to the dirt.

Seeing his opportunity, Benny rushed forward with his spear aimed at Pib.

But the trained defender caught Benny's advance from the corner of his eye and turned just in time to grab the spear, the tip hovering only inches from his throat. Pib gave Benny a smile, knowing this small, black mouse was no match for his strength. He yanked the spear away from Benny's grasp and tossed it to a corner of the room.

However, Benny did not shrink away, and instead, he tackled Pib, sending them both to the ground. Benny landed on top and aimed his claws at Pib's throat. Benny brought down the strike to end the mouse's life . . . but Fib was faster and caught Benny's wrist.

Suddenly, lightning ran through Benny's whole body as Tib's claws found a weak spot in Benny's armor, shredding the flesh on his back.

"Get off me," Pib grunted, shoving Benny to the dirt.

Benny struggled to stand to his feet, but a flurry of kicks from Tib and Fib sent him into a world of pain.

"Stop!" York cried.

The three defenders continued.

"I said stop!"

They obeyed and stood to the side.

Benny's father hobbled forward. Silently, the blind mouse felt over Benny's face. He ripped the helmet off Benny's head and struck his son with the back of his paw. The metallic taste of blood filled Benny's mouth. York struck him again, and again, and again, and again . . .

Gasping for breath, York stepped back from his son. "You'll have to excuse me, Benny. My age is catching up to me."

Benny was a crumpled mess. Barely able to see from one eye, he watched as Pib grabbed the spear from the corner of the room where it had landed. The defender handed Benny's spear to York. The Prophet approached Benny and raised the spear. Tib stepped forward and helped York guide the shaft until the tip rested against Benny's neck.

"Goodbye, Son," York said. "Maybe you'll find your truth."

Suddenly, a spear point erupted from Tib's chest. The three turned to see a bloodied Madison charging them.

York, smelling the rat, pushed Fib and Pib in front of him, shouting, "Defend your prophet!"

The two large mice and Madison clashed. They bit and clawed, foaming spittle flying from their mouths.

Madison grabbed hold of Fib's neck with his fangs, and soon, only Pib remained.

Pib tore a chunk out of Madison's leg, sending the rat to his knees, but before the mouse could finish the job, Madison wrapped his tail around Pib's neck. The mouse was lifted high into the air, clawing at the tail, gasping for breath.

"We only wanted freedom!" Madison roared. There was a loud snap, like the breaking of a twig.

Unfortunately, no sooner had Pib's body landed on the floor, when York seized the opportunity, and charged forward, plunging Benny's spear into Madison's side.

Madison howled, and with his last bit of strength, knocked back York, as well as the bloody spear.

The old rat fell to his side. Blood poured from the spear wound and pooled around his body.

York patted around blindly till he found the spear and charged the old rat again.

Benny summoned the last of his strength, dashed across the room, pulling Madison's spear from Tib's chest. With a great shout, Benny rammed the spear through York's neck.

"It's time to contribute, Father," Benny whispered, releasing the spear and collapsing in exhaustion.

York, gurgling blood, clutched at the spear protruding from his neck and stumbled backwards, falling into a large pile of corn kept in a corner of the burrow.

Like a miniature avalanche, the disturbed kernels at the top of the pile tumbled down and covered York's corpse, until the only thing visible was the shaft of the spear.

The Prophet of Generocity was dead.

Benny dragged himself towards Madison and placed a paw on the rat's side. "Just . . . just hang on. I'll get some bandages and heal you . . . just like you taught me and—"

Madison chuckled, then wheezed in pain. "You can't fix this . . . don't have long."

Benny began to cry. "No . . . no . . ."

A wheeze. "Hope . . ."

Benny leaned forward. "What? Hope? Hope for what?"

Madison lifted a trembling paw and pointed to the corn pile.

Wincing, Benny stood up.

Madison grabbed the mouse's wrist and whispered, "Remember, Benny. You . . . have a choice." With that, the rat released his grasp.

Benny did not know how to respond to the strange statement except to give a nod, signaling he had heard the words. Benny limped over to the pile and began digging through the kernels until he felt something large and solid. He gave it a tug. The object barely shifted.

"Come on, guys," Lily said to the other babes, motioning for them to help her father. They rushed forward and stuck their paws into the corn.

Groaning, Benny and the babes pulled, and the object slowly emerged.

At first, Benny was confused at what he saw. He looked to Madison, hoping for more answers, but the rat's eyes were closed, never to open again.

In an instant, the memories flooded his mind, and it all made sense:

"There is a trail leading from the rats' burrow to the field. It appears they were dragging something . . . something they were hiding."

"No," Benny muttered.

"Think! Did the rats ever say where they got their Old Code?"

"No." He squeezed his eyes shut, trying to cease the thoughts.

"What about the humans? Could you forgive them?"

"No!"

"I was scared if you knew the truth, you would reject everything you learned."

Benny fell to his knees. "No!"

"One day, Avaritia will be faced with a decision. And I fear neither you nor Avaritia will ever be ready."

"No!" Benny cried, his paws upon his head. This couldn't be the truth he had been searching for! Not from them! Not from *them*! It was impossible! They were monsters! They violated everything The Old Code taught! How could this—

Suddenly, Benny felt a paw on his shoulder. He turned and found himself staring up into Moon's sympathetic eyes. She held lifted Lily into her arms.

His mate.

His daughter.

His family.

Moon's loving gaze calmed the storm in Benny's mind, allowing him to think of Madison's last words.

"Remember, Benny. You have a choice."

Chapter 48

The Old Code

Lily ran out of the cornfield shouting her father's name.

Benny just finished tossing the last pawful of dirt onto the mass grave of defenders when his daughter leapt into his arms.

"What is it, Lily? What's wrong?"

The small babe pointed to the field. "Some mice are coming. They look scary!"

Before the rats and mice of Avaritia could take a step to retrieve their weapons, the foreign mice emerged from the stalks. However, this group was different from the one the Avaritians had fought a few days ago; their claws were dull, their eyes darted around fearfully, and each mouse grasped a crudely made spear.

The leader of the pitiful group stepped forward. "We are looking for a mouse named Benny."

Benny recognized the female leader. "Hazel?"

The mouse caught sight of her brother, and the air grew thick with tension as the two sides waited for what would come next.

Hazel and Benny rushed at each other and hugged.

"But how did you get free?" Benny asked.

"There were only a few defenders left. When digging for worms, a slave found this." She motioned to Benny's spear in her paw, the one he had left in Generocity. "We made more and were finally able to fight back."

"The defenders. Are they . . . ?"

By his sister's cold expression, Benny did not need to finish the question.

Moon approached. "So, do you plan on staying?"

"If you will allow us."

Moon glanced at her mate, and Benny knew what had to be done.

He turned and gave a wave of his paw. "Follow me, then. All of you."

The group traveled deep into the forest until they entered a clearing. In this clearing, on a hill, stood a stone with the engraved words: *Two rats greedy to give their all for friends, family, and freedom.*

Passing this stone, the group came upon an enormous pine tree. A doorway led into a chamber inside the trunk.

As the mice crowded into the room, Hazel pointed her spear at the curious object in the center. "What's that?"

Benny placed a paw on the book's black cover and answered:

"Hope."

Made in the USA
Middletown, DE
24 November 2016